To Davi

THE PROTECTORS

THE PROTECTORS

Paul J. Westgate

FOR TASHA,
OUR PROTECTOR

TABLE OF CONTENTS

PROLOGUE

A Small University in New England

The two men moved quietly through the dark shadows of the deserted campus. Carefully avoiding being caught on any security cameras, they crossed through the well-lit parking area to the corner of their target building. Noting there were two cars in the lot even at this late hour, the leader paused to check in with his employer.

"Two cars are in the lot. One is the asset's. The other belongs to Individual C."

After a short pause, his employer responded, "Neutralize C. Retrieve the target. All security systems are offline. The rear door is open."

The leader signaled his team member. They moved through the nearly dark building, checking each room. At the end of the hall, they could see a conference room with the light on. Entering and shutting the door behind them, they saw the asset seated at a table. He looked up and spoke in a hoarse whisper.

"Finally! You'll find the professor in the lab with both dogs. He'll leave soon to take the black Shepherd back to the off-site location. You need to act fast! The dog is in the travel crate and should be easy to get."

"Which lab are they in?"

"The one on the level below us. No one else is in the building."

The leader looked at the man with distaste. He was a whiny, low-level bureaucrat who was monitoring the research program for the Department of Defense. Nervous sweat filled the room with a pungent, repulsive smell. "What about the other dog? The little white one? We were told you investigated her and would provide instructions."

"She's just a puppy. They're trying to train her to see how she compares. She's nothing special. Leave her."

The leader nodded. "Okay, you know what we need to do." As the asset shuddered with apprehension, the other team member stepped up behind him and inserted a needle in his neck. As the man felt consciousness fading away, his last memory was a fist smashing into his nose.

Easing their way out of the stairwell, the two intruders could see lights coming from one of the rooms. The faint sound of tapping on a computer was coming from the doorway.

Using a mirror to look into the room, the two men could see the scientist they knew as Individual C seated at a desk typing notes into a laptop computer.

The leader pointed, and his partner stepped in and quickly plunged the syringe into the professor's neck. Before he could inject the entire dose, he heard a roar. As the huge black dog charged at him, he instinctively threw his hands up to defend himself. The weight of the canine slammed into him, buckling his knees and dropping him to the floor. He felt its jaws close around his neck.

For an instant, the leader stood frozen as the dog burst out of the crate. As he raised his dart gun, he was certain his associate was going to die. To his surprise, the professor called out a sharp command, "STOP!" As the dog released its grip, the leader fired a dart that hit it in the haunch. He quickly retrieved the syringe from the floor and plunged it into the professor's shoulder, administering the remainder of the dose. Still reeling with shock and adrenaline, the two men loaded the dog into its crate and escaped with it out the rear door.

PART 1

Two Years Later

The soccer ball appeared suspended against a blue New England sky. For a moment, it seemed as if time stopped. All eight players watched as it dropped in front of Avika, one of the twelve-year-old team members and the only girl on the field. The 14-year-old players erupted in panic. Although the goal dimensions for this game they called foot hockey were narrow, "Avi" had the most precise kick on the field. And she was wide open.

Her kick resulted in cheers from the older boys as it was clear that it was slightly wide of the net. Their joy was short-lived when they saw Nicolas streaking down the sideline. Even at twelve, "Nico" was the fastest runner on the field. Alex, the proud captain of the "14's," chased frantically after him, but it was too late. After just one bounce, Nico tapped the ball into the net, and the three remaining younger players went wild.

Alex turned and charged toward Noah, the captain of the younger team. Through gritted teeth, he said, "You SLIME!" His hands hit Noah in the chest and threw him backward. As he landed in the soft grass, Noah's first reaction was to look to the sideline. A white German Shepherd was intently watching him. Her body was slightly raised, ears straight up, tail down. Noah quickly put his right hand out even with the ground. As he felt his shirt gather in the larger boy's hand, he saw the dog's body relax.

"You sly fox!" With one hand, Alex lifted Noah. He wrapped his arms around him and squeezed. Noah beamed, "I knew you guys would fall for it."

"So you made this game up just to beat us?"

Noah smiled. "I knew you'd be faster and stronger, but we overcame that with the small goals and the incredible goalkeeping of Diego."

Alex hugged Noah again and pointed at the other three 12-year-olds. "Well, you little scumbags...We'll take your kitchen duties for two weeks per the bet." The other older players shook their heads. Will, the most vocal of the group, exclaimed, "SCREW that!"

Alex looked at him and raised an eyebrow. Will's eyes went to the ground, "Okay, okay.

But remember, you got us into this. You get the pots."

As the older boys walked away, Noah beamed at his friends. "You guys were awesome. I can't believe we pulled this off."

Avi rolled her eyes. "Thank the gods for Diego! Those stops were massive. And Nico, you're like LIGHTNING!"

Nico smiled. "Avi, the placement of that kick was perfect. A few inches either way and Alex would have caught me."

Noah held his left hand down, and the Shepherd trotted over. Avi put her head down, and the dog lightly butted it. "And thank you, Sasha, for all of your moral support." She looked over at Noah. "You heading to the Center?"

Noah nodded. "It's time for our joint language session. Kellen is teaching me to communicate with Sasha." The white Shepherd tilted her head. "Come on! I'm doing better than that." The tilt deepened.

Nico laughed, and Diego smirked. "I guess you better keep at it. We're heading back to the Academy to work on our Chemistry project. See you in class tomorrow."

Noah, Avi, and Sasha watched them walk away. Noah glanced over. "You going to see your mom?" Avi nodded. Her mom, Professor Indira Verma, and Noah's dad, Professor Jens Anderson, had co-founded the Animal Intelligence Initiative. As a leading authority on genetic editing, she was instrumental in convincing the funding organizations to locate the Center at a small, private university. She argued new technologies, like CRISPR, were bringing genetic manipulation to the masses, and it was critical to get in front of the discoveries. The rationale for locating the Center at a low-profile institution was simple: It needed to be out of the public spotlight. This decision would provide the freedom to explore the implications of new science that could modify intelligence.

Noah's dad brought a different focus to the Center. His thesis was genetic changes were only part of the intelligence puzzle. He postulated nurturing, in the form of training and development, was an essential component in the development of intelligence.

In the end, the National Science Foundation (NSF) agreed to support a small Center with one additional scientist, Dr. Kellen Jackson, and a handful of technicians. The Department of Defense (DOD) also provided funding and oversight but maintained a low profile given the nature of the research. The net of all of this was light staffing that resulted in early mornings and late nights being the norm.

For Avi and Noah, it meant they mostly saw her mom and his dad at the Center. As for her father, Avi would visit him at Stanford for two weeks over the summer, and he would come east for Christmas. He and her mom were not on speaking terms. Noah had never known his mother since she passed away shortly after his birth. Noah's and Avi's "free-range" existence was unusual for their age, but it was limited to areas around the University.

Sasha looked up at Noah. Rolling his eyes, he responded, "Okay! Let's go. I know you hate to be late." Looking over at Avi, he whispered, "I think her attentiveness to time comes from her German roots." Seeing her ears tilt back, he added out loud, "I know you can hear us."

The Center

As they approached Professor Verma's office, Avi straightened her clothes and hair. Through the door, Noah could see Avi's mother scrutinizing a paper. Even at 12, Noah recognized she was exceptional in her intelligence and beauty. Intellectually he knew Avi would follow in her mother's footsteps on both fronts, but he still just saw her as his best friend and closest confidant.

The professor looked up and smiled. "Great timing! Come in, please. Sasha, very nice to see you too. How did the game go?"

Noah glanced at Sasha and said, "I'll let Avika tell you all about it." He winked at Avi. "Sasha and I are late to our session with Kellen, and you know how impatient she gets."

"You should take a lesson from her. People need to be respectful of others' time."

Noah agreed. "I know. I know. HEY!" The nip from Sasha got him moving. As he hurried after her down the hall, he called back, "See you tomorrow morning" to Avi.

Two doors down, he turned into the room that served as Kellen's office and laboratory. A gifted athlete, Dr. Kellen Jackson had been an All-American basketball player from Yale who was drafted late in the first round by the Milwaukee Bucks. His family had pitched a fit when he turned the opportunity down to pursue a graduate degree in Behavioral Psychology. After earning his Ph.D., he joined the Center as its first and only staff scientist, shifting his work to understanding non-human body language.

Sitting at his desk, Kellen turned towards the door as he heard the two approach. Focusing first on Sasha, he wrinkled his nose. She responded with a tilt of the head, tail straight back. He shook his head. "Don't worry. He'll grow up. Someday. He's almost on time." As she showed just the hint of teeth, he burst out laughing.

Turning to Noah, he said, "So the plan worked."

"It did. The '14's' took it hook, line, and sinker. Will and James are pissed. I predict attempted retaliation, but Alex will keep them in check."

Kellen raised his eyebrows, "I heard Avi and Nico won the game, but it took Diego's heroics to make it possible."

"True on all points. How did you hear?"

Kellen's smile broadened. "A little birdie told me. But enough, how are you doing with the new vocabulary?"

"It's not very easy."

Sasha shook her head and looked away. Kellen became serious as he walked over and closed the door. Sitting down on a bench, he still towered over the boy. "Noah, you realize how important this is, right?" Receiving the appropriate nod, he continued, "I know you're aware Sasha is special, but I think you need to know just how amazing she is." He looked over at her, and she glanced away. "No, he needs to know and appreciate this."

"Noah, your dad and Professor Verma are on the leading edge of genetically and environmentally modifying intelligence and behavior. Their work with small mammals is considered ground-breaking. But you know many people oppose even this work. We regularly receive death threats, and the lab has been broken into twice."

Noah acknowledged the assessment. "I know. I know. And we modified the large species program to allow only 'natural' breeding processes. Sasha is mostly German Shepherd, a breed known for high intelligence and strong sensing abilities."

Kellen sighed. "That's kind of true. But the extended truth is Sasha is much more than that. Only three people outside of the Department of Defense know this. You can never speak of this to ANYONE outside the Center. No one else can know. Okay?"

Noah agreed, "I already know she's way smarter than any other dog I've met. I've guessed her abilities didn't come from natural breeding." Looking over, Noah could see her watching him with her deep, intelligent eyes. He winked and wrinkled his nose. She responded by lowering her head slightly. Smiling, he added, "I'm pretty sure she's smarter than me."

Kellen agreed. "She certainly has capabilities no human has. She's able to hear frequencies way above the human range. Her sense of smell is among the most acute in dogs. She can sense cues from individuals that indicate nervousness or ill intent. She can also smell the presence of a gun that has been previously fired or cleaned."

Noah said, "But what about her sight? Isn't she essentially color blind?"

Sasha showed her teeth slightly. Kellen laughed. "You're right, Sasha, a common misconception." Turning back to Noah, he continued, "Our work with Sasha shows she can see various shades of blue and yellow. But her real advantage is in low light. Her slight limitations are an inability to focus on very close objects and relatively weak long-distance vision. We have attempted to counteract that in her genetics."

"The real challenge with canines is they tend to only pay attention to objects that are moving." He looked at Sasha. Her ears were up. "Agreed. Your intelligence and our training have overcome this."

Noah turned from Sasha to Kellen. "How modified is she? What would people do if they found out?"

Kellen shrugged. "Professor Verma and your father know the full details, but Sasha is one of only two of her kind. She's part of the Protectors program. It was initiated as a joint effort with the NSF and DOD to address the changing shape of conflict from large-scale warfare to small, terror-focused conflicts. The mission of the initiative is to develop non-human intelligence and security assets. There's a complementary program focused on the use of artificial intelligence and miniaturized robots. But I'm pretty sure the ability to blend in will make animals much more effective, at least for now."

"Noah, what I've just told you has to be kept in strictest confidence. I could be charged with treason, but I feel you needed to know. "

"Absolutely, but you need to tell me one more thing. You said one of two. I never knew there was anyone other than Sasha." Looking over at Sasha, he saw her looking away.

Kellen looked down. His voice broke as he answered. "Ajax was the first. He was a

German Shepherd, like Sasha. We told no one, not even you. He stayed on a farm your father leased. The plan was to have Sasha join him when she was older. We would slip him into the lab at night for tests. He would visit and socialize with Sasha. He and Sasha knew each other for the first six months of her life. He was about two years older. He was kidnapped during a break-in at the lab. Sasha was in the lab, too, but fortunately wasn't taken."

Looking over at Sasha, who still wouldn't look at them, he continued, "We decided to take a different approach with her. We've been hiding her in plain sight. Although no formal announcement was made, we've insinuated she is just the product of selective breeding and intensive training. Her life depends on you keeping this secret."

Noah asked, "Does Avi know this?"

"I don't think so."

Noah paused and then said, "Tell her everything you told me. She needs to know, too."

Kellen agreed. "I will. I promise."

Training Room

The walk to the training room was somber. Kellen attempted to lighten the mood by bringing up the game. "Alright, so remind me how you thought you would beat the '14's'?

Will this actually count as a project for your leadership class?"

Noah smiled. He knew what Kellen was doing and appreciated it. "Well, Professor Feinberg told us we needed to pick a challenge that seemed impossible. When I told her I'd pick four individuals from my grade and beat the notorious jocks, the '14's,' at a physical game, she just laughed and said okay. Your hints about how your Final Four team was so successful helped a lot."

"What role did you play? What concepts did you use from class?"

"I used situational leadership. My teammates had different skills and levels of capability. I had to sense their readiness and treat them differently."

Kellen smiled. "So, think about the elements which apply here."

Noah recalled his earlier lessons. Kellen built his communication program on several principles:

1. Sasha can understand nearly all human language.
2. Humans can use a few non-verbal gestures to communicate confidential information with her.
3. Sasha can communicate a significant number of "words." Like traditional sign language, she augmented the words through her body position.

Noah responded, "Language is conditional. You'll never be able to teach us a complete vocabulary, so I'm going to have to adapt my interpretations based on the situation."

Kellen smiled. "Correct. And you will have to watch Sasha's other body language. Even human language is nuanced and contextual. Sasha's language is more so. For example, a head tilt can mean confusion or disagreement. Add a straight tail to that, and it means strong disagreement."

He glanced at Sasha. "Right?" Her right ear rotated slightly, signaling her agreement.

"Let's review base vocabulary. Sasha, when you're ready."

Sasha went through the 100 new vocabulary words they had learned this month. As she communicated each word using her ears, head position, paws, and tail, Noah called out the meaning. Kellen smiled.

"Noah, you correctly named 96 out of the 100. Let's review those you missed." He called out the four words the boy had gotten wrong, and Sasha replicated them. Noah took pictures and added notes to record them in his tablet.

Kellen raised an eyebrow. "But now let's see how this really works." They walked to the end of the room, where there was a simulated living room set up. "Sasha, please evaluate the room."

Sasha walked into the area. Noah recognized her "alert" stance. He watched as she lowered her right ear and exposed her teeth. Tail back, she carefully scanned the room.

"Noah, what's she telling you?"

"She's saying we should be cautious. There could be danger here."

"Close, but what is the situation telling you? What is her body language saying, not just her signs?"

"I'm not sure...."

A third voice, as even and smooth as glass with a slight Nordic accent, said, "That is not good enough."

Recognizing the tone and cadence, Noah responded, "Dad! Did she know you were here?" before Professor Anderson stepped into view.

"Of course she did. She also sensed there is a recently fired gun inside the end table by the couch. She was signaling danger and aggression. You may have been confused since her response may have been muted because she recognized it was me in the room."

His steel-gray eyes locked on Sasha. "Could this be true?"

Sasha tilted her head. Her tail was down.

"Very well. I am disappointed in the outcome but do not see it as a complete failure. She recognized danger, and you were able to interpret her communication partially. You both must work harder. Please, let us try again. Kellen, do you have another scenario?"

Kellen handed the professor a card:

Case 2 A and B
Two deliveries will be made to the house: One is real, and the other is an abduction.

Case 2 A. The real delivery is a UPS driver.

Case 2 B. The potential abductor is disguised as a pizza delivery driver.
    The only weapon is a knife, undetectable.
    The intent is to take the boy and kill the dog.

A knock sounded on the door to the training area. Noah asked, "Who is it?" while looking through the peephole.

A man's voice could be heard. "Delivery, Sir. I need someone to sign for it. Should only take a second."

Noah looked at Sasha. She stood alert with her ears forward but displayed no other signs. Noah fastened the chain, and as he opened the door, replied, "Just pass it through, please. My dad doesn't want me to let people in when he's not here."

The man handed a clipboard through. Noah signed the form and gave it back. The voice said, "Thanks, I'll leave the package by the door." Footsteps could be heard as he walked away.

Kellen said, "In this next scenario, you're at home waiting for pizza delivery. Ready?" Noah and Sasha both nodded. Kellen grinned; nodding wasn't part of her trained vocabulary.

A doorbell rang. Noah called out, "Who is it?" while looking through the peephole. He could see an attractive young woman wearing shorts and a Vinny's t-shirt, Noah's favorite pizza joint. She was holding a box, nonchalantly chewy gum. "Ya pizza's here."

Noah glanced at Sasha. Her teeth were bared, and her ears were back. Noah dropped his left hand with his two fingers down, signaling Protocol 2, which called for a quiet escape. Kellen smiled as the professor said, "Very good. How did she know?"

Kellen's answer was tentative. "I'm not completely sure. I believe it's something in the girl's voice that signals bad intent. But I've also tried it with the individual being given access to the room without speaking. Sasha correctly identified the assailant every time. In that case, we believe it's body language. We gave her twenty 'reals' in a row before throwing in an 'assailant,' and she got it right away. I can't be certain this will play out in the real world, but I feel the odds are extremely high."

The professor replied, "Very good. But Noah, in the first scenario, you did not need to open the door. She might have been wrong." As Sasha showed her teeth slightly, Kellen attempted to hide his smile.

Home

Noah gathered his gear and prepared for the walk home. "Geez, Sasha, two hours of scenarios. I'm exhausted. How do you think we did, pretty good?" The slight tilt of her head and flick of her left ear made Noah roll his eyes. "You're as bad as Dad." As they exited the building, he asked, "Short cut through the Block?" Seeing her reaction, he pushed. "C'mon, it will save almost ten minutes of walking."

The Block was a small section of town bordering the university and the academy. They were supposed to avoid it by staying on the grounds of the two institutions. Noah viewed it as pretty tame as it only housed a few fast-food restaurants and shops to support the local schools.

Noah muttered, "Screw it," and started walking toward the street. The nip on the back of his leg elicited a "Hey, back off mad dog," but failed to stop him. Growling, Sasha fell in line next to him. "Look, you'll thank me when we get home. Plus, I'm picking up a slice along the way. You want anything?"

Both Noah and Sasha knew a nutritious, if somewhat dull, dinner was waiting for them at home. Professor Anderson was meticulous in his attention to all of their diets. Pizza was grudgingly allowed once a week.

As Noah cut through the alley behind Vinny's, he sensed Sasha's steps change as she suddenly went to full alert. Her deep-throated growl stopped him in his tracks. A man stepped out from behind a dumpster about fifteen feet in front of them.

"Hey Kid, can you spare any change?"

Noah quickly looked over his shoulder, where, to his dismay, another man had turned the corner and was approaching them from behind. They were effectively trapped. He started to signal Sasha when he saw her charge the man in front of them. The distance between her and the man vanished in a flash. Eighty pounds of fury slammed into the man's chest, knocking him off his feet. Her jaws closed on his throat.

"DON'T MOVE!" Noah glanced back and saw the other man had vanished. The man on the ground whimpered. Noah continued, "She's going to release you and back up. If you make any aggressive move, she'll put you down for good, and I can't stop her."

The man gasped, "Okay! Just don't let her kill me." Noah noticed a wet spot on the man's pants and smelled urine.

Sasha released his throat and stepped back, never letting her guard down. The man rubbed his neck and took two steps back before turning and running down the alley. Trotting a couple of steps, Sasha looked down at the assailant's knife laying on the ground. "Crap! How did you know?" Her sharp look was response enough. His hands shaking,

Noah carefully picked it up and tossed it into the dumpster.

"Let's get home."

They walked for several minutes in silence. As they turned the corner to walk to the end of the cul-de-sac, Noah finally spoke. "Sasha, I'm so sorry. You were right. We aren't supposed to take the shortcut.... I'm, I'm an idiot."

Sasha kept walking forward and turned into their driveway. "Wait!" She turned and looked at him as he tried to catch up. "I have to tell Dad, don't I? I know he'll be mad at you, too. I'm so sorry." He sat down on the front step and lowered his head. She came up and gently put her head against his. Noah stood and brushed away a tear.

Picking up the Healthy Meals delivery box, Noah wearily climbed the front steps. He opened the door by placing his hand against a scanning panel. As he entered, he marveled at how this house and everything in his world was a reflection of his father. Born outside of Copenhagen to a German mother and Danish father, Jens grew up at the KTH Royal Institute of Stockholm where both of his parents had exceptional academic careers in the Mechanical Engineering Department. Jens and his sister had inherited their parents' practicality and sense of order. The Anderson home was only 1300 square feet. Everything seemed to be in the exact place it belonged and utilized the latest technology. Jens expected the same level of precision from his son. Disappointing him was one of Noah's greatest fears. Having it somehow seem Sasha's fault cut through him like a knife.

Fixing Sasha's dinner of chicken and rice, Noah shot off a text to Avika.

N: Hey. Bad news. Incident on walk home.

The response took only moments.

A: Mom just heard. Your dad knows and is on his way.

Noah's stomach dropped as he heard the Volvo pull into the garage.

N: Here. Going.

A: Luck!

As the door opened, Noah tried to get ahead of the situation. "Dad, it was all my fault. Let me explain." His father just held up his hand. In a rare show of emotion, he wrapped Noah up in his left arm. He put his right out to Sasha, who came over against his leg. Without a word, he held them close. After a long moment, he drew back.

"Police came to the lab and showed me footage from Vinny's capturing the incident. Your pizza habit paid off because the workers recognized you on the video. You should have called me immediately. The police are on their way over to question you. You're not in trouble with them or me. Yes, I am disappointed you ignored my instructions to never walk through the Block. But you are a boy, and I realize you may make poor decisions occasionally. I hope this prevents some in the future."

Looking at Sasha, he continued, "As for you, young lady, I believe those men were hired to abduct you or Noah. You must not let his impulsive nature lead you into danger. Please be more assertive with him."

He drew them close for a moment, then released when the security system's feminine voice announced, "Police officers arriving momentarily." To silence the announcement, he responded, "Noted."

They met them in the driveway. A female officer stepped out of the driver's side of the vehicle, and a large male emerged from the passenger's side. The woman spoke first. "Professor Anderson, as you recall, I'm Sergeant Murphy. This is my partner, Officer Janes."

As he acknowledged them, he said, "This is my son, Noah."

Officer Janes spoke up. "Where's the dog?"

"She's inside the house."

"Can we go in and see her?"

"No, you may not."

"She was involved in an incident where she bit someone. You were supposed to report it."

Noah's father turned to face Officer Janes. His gray eyes held the officer's as he said evenly, "Your department reported the incident to me based on video footage and a call from the Pizzeria. It would seem to me you should be more concerned with the armed mugging Sasha prevented. If you wish to ask my son questions about that, I will permit it. If you continue with this aggressive stance, I will ask you to leave and then contact our lawyer."

Sergeant Murphy came forward. "Janes, take a step back." He hesitated and then reluctantly did so as she glared at him. Turning to Noah, she asked, "Can you tell us what happened?"

Noah described the encounter. Murphy interjected with a couple of questions. When Janes attempted to intercede, she just put up a hand. Noah hesitated when he got to the end but then admitted he threw the knife in the dumpster.

Murphy stepped away to talk into her radio. Janes took this as an opportunity to question Noah. "How do we know the knife wasn't already there?"

Murphy came back before Noah could answer. "The men on the scene found the knife. We'll check for prints, but I doubt we'll find anything. The second perp didn't show up on the video, but I will provide your description."

She looked at Noah's father, "We're documenting this as a mugging gone bad. If the knife hadn't been found, this could've gone very differently."

The professor asked, "Do you have any additional questions?" When she shook her head, he said, "Please leave us now."

As they left, Jens turned to Noah. "Officer Janes is not to be trusted. We should always be cautious around agents of the government. They are not all as they seem."

They turned and walked back to the house. Dinner was eaten in near silence. Noah knew this was not unusual with this father, but he sensed something deeper was troubling him. After cleaning up the dishes, Noah announced he and Sasha would be in his room completing his homework and then straight off to bed.

His father stated, "I will work in the home office this evening if you need me for anything." Looking to Sasha, Noah gave an almost imperceptible nod. She also sensed his father was concerned.

In his room, working on his Linear Algebra homework, Noah heard his phone chirp. It was a text from Avika.

A: How'd it go? Everything ok?

N: Dad's upset, happy we're safe.

A: Police?

N: Weird vibes.

A: Talk?

N: Not tonight. Waaay behind.

A: K. Tomorrow.

The Academy

Noah and Sasha reached the meeting spot just after Avika. He could see Nico and Diego half a block away. Before they arrived, Avi quietly asked, "Everything good?"

Noah nodded, and Sasha gave a single tail wag. "Dad was really shaken up. The police asked a bunch of questions. One was a woman. She was in charge, a Sergeant or something. She seemed okay. The other was this strange guy. He wanted to see Sasha. My dad wouldn't let him and definitely didn't trust him."

Avi waved as the two boys walked up. Diego frowned at Noah and said, "Word is the police were at your house last night." Nico added, "So what's going on?"

As they walked to the Academy, Noah recounted the story. After a glance from Sasha, he downplayed her role slightly, leaving out the part of her jaws on the man's neck. A slight motion from her tail and the position of her ears showed her approval. When he got to the point with the knife, Diego stepped ahead and turned to Noah. The group stopped.

"That's serious stuff. What do you think he wanted?"

Noah paused and involuntarily glanced at Sasha. "I don't know, but probably money for drugs or something." He looked at Avi, who was also giving him the "shut this down" look. He added, "Look, guys, let's not mention the knife when people ask us about it, okay? I don't want it to be a big deal. I just want to forget about it."

As the group agreed, Nico said, "You got it. But the real question is, what are we going to do with our free hour this afternoon?" The thought of six hours of free time over the next two weeks brought smiles all around.

The Academy, founded by a group of professors, was hosted by a private school adjacent to the university. Private donors provided funding to ensure its independence, but the budget was always tight. As a result, students conducted many of the services required for day-to-day operation. Duties rotated, and all students had to work in the kitchen and other areas, such as grounds keeping. The Founders agreed this built character, and no one was exempt from working three hours per week. Kitchen clean-up, the most dreaded duty, was the frequent currency of bets between students.

As they reached the tall iron gates at the school's entrance, they saw the imposing figure of Kellen glancing at his watch.

"You guys are running behind. You better hurry to beat the bell!"

Morning classes were joint with the private school. The instructors seemed to relish having a reason to call out Academy participants who were often younger than the other students. Sasha and Kellen watched as the four of them hurried off to their first classes.

As they turned to walk back to the lab, Kellen spoke softly. "Near miss last night." He watched Sasha's response. "True, but you won't be able to prevent all of his foolish inclinations. Ultimately, I think it was a valuable experience for both of you." Seeing her look, he snorted. "Well, I didn't say pleasant."

Noah managed to grind his way through his first two classes. Unlike Avi, who could maintain focus through any lecture, he had to fight to listen during Algebra and Chemistry. He found himself staring out the window, wondering how Sasha's day was going. Several times his instructors called on him, expecting to catch him unaware and answerless. In each case, he provided the correct response and settled back into his daydreams. Finally, the bell for the third period, Physical Education, sounded.

Even though he, Diego, and Nico were younger than the other boys, they all loved gym. And when Mr. Mitchell announced today's class was five-on-five bombardment, they knew it was going to be a fun day. Alex and Will, the two most athletic older boys, were selected as Captains. When Will picked first, he predictably chose Dave, another 14-year-old. When Alex immediately took Noah, the other older boys smirked. They laughed out loud when he added Nico and Diego with his following two selections. With his last pick, Noah convinced him to take Joe. Due to his size and awkwardness, Joe was often picked last. He also openly admitted he was not very fast, but Noah knew Joe had a secret.

"Hey, Alex, want to adjust the bet?" Will's confidence oozed out of him.

Alex looked over his team and turned back, "Nope. If you guys were to win, I'd clean the kitchen by myself. When we win, I'm off for the next three sessions."

Will and Dave laughed and rolled their eyes.

Mr. Mitchell reviewed the rules. "When I blow the whistle, everyone can run to get the three volleyballs in the middle of the basketball court. If you're hit, you're out. If you catch a ball, the person throwing it is out. If you step past the free-throw line on the opponent's side, you're out. Got it?" Nods all around as the teams headed to the opposite ends of the court.

Noah gathered the team around and said, "Nico, we need you to get to the two left balls and kick them back. Get the balls to Alex and Joe." Diego looked skeptical. "Trust me. And Alex, remember what I told you."

At the whistle, Nico raced to the center and sent the two balls back. He ran out of the way as Will got the third ball. Surprisingly, Will ignored Nico and charged toward Noah. "This is for kitchen duty!" He wound up and slammed the ball into Noah from only ten feet away. As Noah fell, Will's smile was wiped off his face by a ball thrown by Alex. Nico retrieved the ball and tossed it back to Alex. The four remaining members of his team now advanced to the opposing foul line with all three balls.

From the sideline, Noah called, "Only Joe throws!" Alex shook his head but then said, "FINE! This better work."

As Joe came up to the line, he wound up and released the ball. When it hit the back wall, it sounded like the gym shook. His arm was like a cannon. After several near misses, Dave decided to try to catch one of his throws. The ball came at him dead center and slammed his hand aside. As the ball started to roll away, his teammate to the left attempted to grab it only to get hit in the back by Joe. One of the remaining members of Will's team managed to grab one of the balls and hit Joe.

The two remaining members of Will's team advanced as Diego, Alex, and Nico quickly retreated. The two older boys unleashed a withering series of throws that pinned their opponents against the wall. Watching carefully, Diego waited for the right moment, and when one of the balls flew toward him, he stepped in and caught it. He tossed it to Alex, who quickly bounced it off the back of the remaining opponent.

Alex walked over to Will. "Have fun this afternoon." Will and his teammates walked away, dejected. Turning to Noah, he said, "How do you do that? How did you know it would work?"

Noah shrugged. "It kind of feels natural. But I do admit, I know Joe's been compared to a young CC Sabathia, and he'll try out for varsity baseball this year."

Joe grinned shyly, "It's the only sport I enjoy playing. Noah and I talked about it once. I told him, I can't run, but I can throw."

As they walked out of the gym, Alex clapped Joe on the shoulder. "You sure as heck can throw. Will is so pissed." The three boys laughed.

After their third class, Academy members separated from the rest of the students. They walked to a small building in the corner of the complex adjacent to the University. Here they took the unique courses that together comprised the Academy curriculum. The classes were typically small and taught by professors or other individuals with unique capabilities.

Professor Rachel Feinberg was highly sought after in the Leadership and Change Management field. Her class was a favorite at the Academy. She taught only one session a year and accepted only four students. Attendees of her similar college course often went on to become CEOs, political power brokers, or in one case, a captain who led his team to the Final Four. Noah knew all this, but for him, it was just a lot of fun.

Professor Feinberg discussed a wide range of concepts. She believed that leadership could not be learned or trained, but it could be nurtured and enhanced. If done correctly, good leaders would rise. The question was how far and what might derail them. She did not rely on strict lectures or tests and preferred to assign projects to hone students' skills in real situations.

Noah and his classmates, Avi, Alex, and a young woman named Beth, had applied numerous leadership theories in mock settings in the classroom and had discussed these models in light of their previous experiences. Noah's application of Situational Leadership to the game with the "14's" had been his first real-life project. As he walked into the door, he could see the professor was eager to discuss the outcome.

"So, Noah, how did the foot hockey game go?"

Alex glared at Noah. "You mean that was a project? For this class?"

Noah explained, "I needed to keep it from the rest of you to prevent the results from being affected." Turning back to Professor Feinberg, he said, "Obviously, we won."

The Professor smiled, "Excellent! Let's discuss how you did it."

"The first thing I did was evaluate my assets and develop a strategy. I used a simple version of the Strengths, Weaknesses, Opportunities and Threats Approach."

He projected a graphic from his laptop onto the room's screen:

Key Strengths:
- ✓ **Ability to defend (Diego)**
- ✓ **Speed (Nico)**
- ✓ **Accuracy (Avi)**

After highlighting each strength, Noah continued, "But I knew our primary Weakness was our smaller size. The Opportunity was to skew the game in our favor by using small nets and a short playing time. We could then leverage our Strengths to win with a single goal at the end of the game. The Threat was we would get enticed to try to score earlier and get drawn into the opponent's style of game."

Professor Feinberg agreed, "It seems like a sound strategy." She turned to Alex, "Did you realize what was happening?"

Alex rolled his eyes, "We had no idea. When we realized time was running out, we attacked the goal. I didn't believe they could get it by us. We were stunned when they scored, and we lost."

She turned to Avi, "How did you feel before the game?"

Avi shook her head, "Well, everyone knows Noah takes the lead. We were surprised he proposed the game, but I was shocked when he turned over big parts of the preparation to Diego. But it all felt natural once it started coming together. I never felt I was being 'managed.' I went into the game believing we could win."

Turning her focus back to Noah, she asked, "What was the greatest challenge?"

"Convincing my team that we could do this. I applied the principles of Situational Leadership. Diego was an S-4, completely ready to tend goal, so it was easy to delegate that to him. Avi and Nico were less ready." He glanced over at Avi, who was frowning at him.

"How did you characterize them, and what did you do?"

"On some skills, like Nico's speed and Avi's kicks, they were ready but not confident. I tried to be supportive and let them decide how we would apply their capabilities. I guess they were S-3s. But on other skills, like how to defend, none of us except Diego were ready. He took the leadership role and had us watch highlights from Germany's 2014 World Cup team. Under his direction, we practiced specific skills and agreed to stick with the strategy. I had him treat us like S-2s."

Professor Feinberg smiled. "This was excellent work. Noah, I'm happy to see you incorporate these principles into your everyday life. I've heard you extended the lesson in gym class today. You all seem to really get it. Okay, now let's shift our attention to a different leadership challenge, Change Management..."

The Center

Sasha's day was structured much like Noah's. Throughout the morning, she had classes on human language, maps and locations, and math. Kellen had created a learning system that adapted self-taught online courses for her purposes. Using equipment designed to enable basic navigation on the computer, she worked through the lessons prescribed, but like Noah, she longed to get out of her classroom.

Relief came when Kellen arrived at the door, ready to go out for a run. "I got a notification you finished, and I'm dying to get outside." Sasha bounded up and bumped Kellen with her head. As they walked outside, he added, "One thing you should know, I've asked the assistants to set up 'encounters' on the run.

In each case, you'll need to react and communicate with me, but let's try not to hurt them."

As they started the run, Sasha's proud bearing and easy gait communicated she wasn't concerned. Throughout the five-mile course, she aced every situation they encountered. She trotted along as if the eight minutes per mile pace was a stroll in the park. Kellen marveled at how the little puppy he had met just three years ago had developed into this extraordinary individual who he considered his best and most trusted friend. The sacrifices he had made, the long hours, missed vacations, and total lack of personal life, despite attempts of women at the university to "set him up," all seemed insignificant as he watched her.

As the run wound down, they walked back to the Center and Sasha caught him watching her. The tilt of her head was met with his smile. "I was just thinking how you used to have a hard time keeping up with me." Seeing her reaction, he laughed. "You're right. That was a long time ago."

Reaching his office, he saw a message in capital letters on his whiteboard: CONFERENCE ROOM 3:00! The note continued in smaller letters below: From now on, ALWAYS bring your cell phone anywhere you go.

Retrieving his cell phone from his desk drawer, he saw he had missed several texts from Jens and one from Noah. He responded to Jens' text first.

J: Where are you?

J: Meeting at 3:00.

K: Was running, will be there.

Next, he checked and responded to Noah's text.

N: Dad reached out. What's up?

K: Unknown, meeting at 3.

The response came back immediately.

N: Avi and me too.

The conference room was between Professors Anderson and Verma's offices. Noah and Avi entered the room together. The window shades were down, and their parents were already seated at the end of the conference table. Moments later, promptly at 3:00 PM, Sasha and Kellen entered. Professor Anderson stood and closed the door. Professor Verma clicked a switch on an unknown device on the table and started the conversation.

"This instrument will block all known forms of listening devices. What we're about to discuss must never leave this room. Does everyone agree?" Nods all around, including Sasha. "Good. Jens, would you please tell us what you have found?"

Noah's dad stood, and the screen at the end of the table illuminated. "This morning, between 3:05 and 3:25 AM, someone was watching our house. As you can see, we were unable to capture any definitive images. It would appear he's aware of our cameras and motion detectors. He is not aware of our more sophisticated night vision sensors, which recorded his presence and allowed us to see these images."

"But Dad, we barely see anything. How do you even know he's a male?"

Professor Anderson zoomed in on one of the frames that clearly showed the outline of a large man. "We have enhanced this image. Based on the tree beside him, we know his height is between 74 and 75 inches, and based on his body dimensions, his weight is between 220 and 240 lbs."

"That's Officer Janes!"

Professor Anderson held up his right hand. "We have considered this." A picture of Janes in front of their house appeared next to the image. "But our evidence is not conclusive. And please wait. There is more to discuss. Between 3:30 and 3:50 this morning, an individual was also detected outside the Verma's home." A third image appeared on the screen, but it was even less distinct. "It's highly likely this is the same individual. This realization made us suspect the surveillance is tied to the Center and not to yesterday's incident with Noah and Sasha." He turned to Professor Verma. "Indira?"

She brought up a schematic of the Center with several locations marked with L's or C's. "Based on these conclusions, we decided to do a thorough sweep of the Center for observation devices. We found four listening devices and two cameras." She pointed to their locations. We have debated the merits of removing the devices versus letting them stay. In the end, we have decided none are in areas where they are likely to capture confidential information. We'll leave them as-is for now, so we do not tip off our observers that we have found them."

She glanced at Professor Anderson, who continued. "This means we need to use extreme care to not discuss anything outside the confines of the lab, the offices, or this conference room. We are also reinforcing that anyone who enters these areas must follow the security protocols. Our belief is the cleaning crew was compromised since the planted devices are only in areas they can access. We're pursuing this hypothesis."

Kellen asked, "Jens, are you sure the lab and offices are clean?"

The professor replied, "Our friends from the DOD have stopped by to do a sweep. They completed the lab while you were on your run."

Avi piped up, "What do you think they are after? Are we safe on campus? What should we do?"

Her mom explained, "It appears they are interested in the research we are conducting at the lab. As you know, various groups are adamantly against our work to develop genetically modified animals. We have attempted to be discrete, but word did get out a few years ago based on a fabricated story we think originated from someone in one of our funding agencies." She flashed a picture on the screen of a tabloid article titled, "HYPERINTELLIGENT RATS ESCAPE UNIVERSITY LAB."

"The other possibility is a foreign agent has become aware of our work and would like to steal it. The scarier proposition is they may attempt to kidnap one of us to extract what we know. Alternatively, they may try to go after you for leverage. There is also a slim chance they are aware of Sasha's capabilities. In short, there are many possibilities. For now, we should assume we're relatively safe on campus, but even there, do not walk alone and always carry your phone."

Kellen glanced at Sasha, and seeing the question she was communicating, he directed it to Professor Anderson. "Sasha is wondering if we feel it's safe for just her and the children to be away from campus."

As Noah's father started to speak, Avi's mother cut him off. "No! On no terms are either of you to be off-campus without an adult." Turning to Sasha, her tone softened, "I know you can protect them, but I feel it creates too tempting of a target." Sasha's single tail thump signaled her agreement.

Professor Anderson added one more thing. "We also would like the three of you to work with Kellen on how to avoid potential situations and to learn basic self-defense. Based on what's happened recently, he has asked a friend who we have already checked out and can be trusted to help. You will meet with her starting tomorrow afternoon."

Home - Days Later

Noah was finishing the last of his homework when he heard the chime.

A: Talk?

He clicked on Avi's picture, and she appeared on his right monitor.

"Geez, Kellen and Mary were brutal today, right?"

Noah nodded in agreement. His body ached all over from the strength and endurance training that had become their afternoon ritual.

"Yeah, when Dad said we'd learn self-defense, I wasn't thinking we were starting basic training."

Avi agreed. "Mary's quite interesting, though. Her lectures on 'Prevention is the Best Defense' are pretty thought-provoking. And she seems intent to drill it into us that fighting back is the option of last resort."

Noah frowned. "Yeah, based on what I know now, I would have never gotten into the situation in the alley." He glanced over at Sasha, who was watching and listening from her bed. "I know. If I had listened to you in the first place..."

Turning back to Avi, he added, "Hey, did you catch when Mary said some of the escape moves come from Jiu-Jitsu and others from Krav Magra?"

"I did. Kellen seems intent on us never having to use them, though. His interval training is killing me. Only Sasha can keep up." Calling out louder, "Sasha, can't you wear him down more in your morning runs?"

Seeing her reaction, Noah replied, "She says he already can't keep up with her. She doesn't want to embarrass him."

When their laughter died down, Noah said, "See you in the morning."

The Academy

For over a month, there were no further incidents. Noah and Avi were beginning to feel like the earlier incidents were aberrations, and things were back to normal. They continued to follow their parents' instructions, but their diligence in maintaining strict awareness of their surroundings and only staying in secure areas on campus became lax. This sudden realization came to Noah as he and Avi passed between two campus buildings late one evening after studying in the library. He saw Sasha go into full alert.

With a quick hand signal, he communicated "message received" and ensured Avi was aware something was wrong. He signaled a 2, indicating Protocol 2, and then a fist that defined their agreed-upon meeting point after their split. Avi said a soft okay, and he saw Sasha turn her right ear slightly in acknowledgment.

As Avi suddenly sprinted to her right, Noah ran in the opposite direction toward a dumpster behind the building. He felt a presence behind him and glanced back to see a man appear from behind a bush. The cool air rushed over him as Noah hurdled a barely visible pipe jutting out from the wall. The stranger chasing him didn't see it in time and slammed his knee directly into it. Cursing, the man dropped to the ground as Noah reached the dumpster. Hesitating to look back, he suddenly felt a hand on his shoulder.

"Gotcha! Just come with us, and nothing bad will hap, OOF!!"

The man's words were cut off as Sasha slammed into him. Her deep-throated growl was followed by a crunching noise. The man cried out in pain as he held his broken hand. Noah pulled away and ran behind the dumpster as he watched Sasha disappear into the shadows as she headed in Avi's direction. He found the small space in the fencing he and Sasha had seen during a previous walk near the building. Noah pushed his way through the tight opening just as his pursuer came around the dumpster. When he was almost through, his shirt caught one of the broken loops. The man reached through the tight gap, grabbing his belt. Pulling as hard as he could, Noah heard and felt the shirt tear. His hand touched the ground and landed on a fist-sized stone. As he felt himself being pulled back through the fence, he twisted and swung the stone in an arc, hoping to knock the man's hand free. The stone missed the pursuer's hand but connected directly with his face. Noah paused for just an instant, amazed at the amount of blood streaming from the man's nose.

Gathering his wits, Noah sprinted off toward the meeting point. As he came out of the darkness, he saw Sasha appear next to him. He whispered, "Clear?" to which she gave a confirmation. Then he asked, "Avi?" Sasha signaled no. She hadn't seen her on her prescribed path but hadn't detected followers.

Noah entered the code, and they slid into the storage area for the Paleobiology Department. He whispered, "Good thing Dad is friends with Dr. Johansson, and we got access to this. Avi should show up soon."

As they waited, he quickly shot a text to his dad.

N: Code RED!

J: Stay put. On our way.

As they waited, Noah became impatient. "Where's Avi? She should be here by now!" Turning on his tracking app, he could see the location of her phone. He felt his stomach drop as he realized the phone was nearby but was moving away. Sasha, glancing only briefly at his screen, moved to the door. When he stood to go with her, she bristled. "You can't find her without me." Seeing her response, he added, "They'll be too late. They're coming but are at least ten minutes away." She hesitated, and then they both went out the door.

Across Campus

After Noah gave the signal, Avi had sprinted around the building. She heard some noises from his direction, but she continued to the meeting point per their agreement. Seeing some students walking toward her desired destination, she fell in line and tried to appear to be one of them.

The issue came when the students turned away from the meeting point. She could either stay with them and then attempt to contact Noah or cut across the Quad to get to the Paleobiology building. Confident no one had followed her, she started walking across the Quad. Halfway to the other side, a man seemed to appear out of nowhere. Turning back, she saw a second pursuer approaching from behind.

Sprinting off the path and away from the men, Avi felt confident she would be able to lose them. She gave a burst of speed as one of the men threw something at her. Avi felt something smash into her legs and wrap around her feet. Unable to move, she fell forward. Trying to break the fall with her hands proved futile. Her head hit the ground, and the world went black.

Noah and Sasha followed Avi's phone signal as it moved away from the rendezvous point. When they finally caught up, Noah had to fight back a gasp. Two men were carrying Avi toward a delivery truck parked behind the Mathematics building. Staying in the shadows, Noah pulled out his phone and typed two quick messages to his dad and Kellen.

N: Code Black!

N: Track Avi!

As Noah and Sasha watched from the shadows, two additional men approached the van. One seemed to be limping a bit, and there was no mistaking the other. Even from this distance in the low light, Noah could see something wrapped around his hand and the blood on his face. He heard his phone chirp a response.

J: On our way. Stand down.

Noah looked at Sasha and saw her response before he asked the question. The two of them were no match for the group. Looking back, he noticed two of the men were looking in his direction. He glanced down and realized they could probably see the glow from his phone. To his dismay, he also saw the other two men looking at something, and then looking at his tracking app, he saw Avi's phone signal disappear.

He looked back to Sasha, who was giving the signal to flee. As the men started running toward them, he and Sasha ran in opposite directions. Hoping to keep the men in the area longer, he slowed slightly and remained visible. To his surprise, he saw the men stop and turn back to the van.

As Avi regained consciousness, she heard men talking. She was lying on a cold surface and felt zip ties around her wrists and ankles. Her head hurt, and it felt hard to focus. Opening her eyes slightly, she could see her abductors looking at her phone. Seeing the screen go black, she guessed they shut it off to prevent tracking. Focusing on their voices, she could make out some of their words.

"....got one of the targets. What happened to the other?"

"Fought like a devil. My hand's broken. I think my nose is, too."

"Look over there, what's that?"

Two of the men started sprinting away. The injured man called out a muted, "STOP." As the two runners returned, she missed his first words, but the last part of the message was clear and sent chills up her spine.

"....have what we need. Let's get her out of here."

Avi kept her eyes shut as she heard steps approaching. A voice said, "No need to pretend. I saw you moving. And nothing to worry about. We don't want to hurt you." She felt hands lift her and place her on something soft in the back of the truck. For a moment, Avi thought about her mom and Noah wondering where she was, and she felt tears in her eyes.

Avi bit her lip and told herself to be tough. She pictured Sasha so stoic and proud and vowed to emulate her. Glancing at her watch, Avi noted the time. Based on the travel time and an estimate of the truck's speed, she could guess some of the places they might take her. She felt a light wrap being draped over her. "Let me know if you get too hot or cold."

Noah heard Kellen's car as it turned the corner. Almost simultaneously, he saw the police car, lights flashing, coming from the other direction. When Kellen and his dad ran over, Noah couldn't help himself. Between sobs, he said, "They took her! She's gone." He saw Sergeant Murphy get out of the car. The world seemed to spin, and then he felt his father's hand on his shoulder.

Murphy's voice was urgent. "Noah, you need to focus. Tell us everything that happened. We will find Avi, but you need to stay strong."

Noah looked at Murphy and then glanced at Sasha. Getting the okay that showed Sasha sensed no ill intent, he started to describe the encounter. Murphy interrupted and said, "Noah, first describe the van. I want to get an APB and Amber Alert out ASAP."

Noah described the delivery van. "Did you see the license plate?" He shook his head and then looked at Sasha. Watching her closely, Noah observed her signals and then replied, "I think it contained the letters HRE."

Murphy said, "Give me a minute. I'll be right back." As they waited, Avi's mom's car raced into the lot. Jumping out, she looked to Noah's father.

"Where is she?"

"We don't know. We are working on it."

She came forward, and as she started to stumble, Kellen put his arm around her. Distraught, she fell against his chest.

Murphy came back and said, "The Techs are on their way. I want us to move away from this area in case there's anything they can find." After they all moved away from where the van had parked, she focused on Noah and demanded, "Tell us everything you remember. Focus. The details matter."

As Noah recalled the event, he looked to Sasha and then would make minor adjustments. He described the encounters, the men, and what they were wearing. Murphy interjected with short questions to clarify but tried not to interrupt the flow. When Noah finished, she went back and asked detailed questions and added additional notes to her pad. When he described the man getting injured, she got on her radio, and they heard her direct another team to the location where Noah was almost caught.

When she was finished with Noah, Murphy turned to Avi's mother and Noah's father. "Do you know anyone who might have a reason to abduct your children?" The parents glanced at each other.

PART 2

A Distant Warehouse

As the van came to a stop, Avi completed her calculation. Based on her rough estimates, they had traveled 35 to 45 miles in 70 minutes. She was also confident two-thirds of the travel was on highways, which meant they had likely gotten on the Turnpike. As she listened, Avi could hear the distant hum of vehicles, confirming they were still within a mile of the highway. Based on her knowledge of the local road systems, she could narrow her location down to three or four towns.

When her abductors finally opened the van's rear doors, cool air rushed over her, and she could smell pine trees nearby. Avi felt a pang of fear when she realized they were not concerned their faces were visible. They all looked pretty non-descript, and when the one who seemed to be the leader asked, "Are you okay?" she detected a slight Eastern European accent. Nodding as they came into the van, her eyes went wide as he pulled out a long knife. He smiled and quickly cut the restraints around her ankles.

"Don't do anything silly like try to run or scream. No one will hear you, and you will just anger our employer."

"Who's your employer? Why am I here?"

He just smiled and helped her step down from the van. She noticed they were behind a warehouse that appeared to be abandoned. The land behind them was wooded, and, other than the distant highway, there were no sounds or other clues as to where they were. After entering the warehouse, he led her down a hall that had several doors on both sides. Several of them were marked with colored circles. Passing by closed doors with blue and black circles, they entered a door denoted by a pink circle.

Inside the room was a small bed, desk, and chair. A flat-screen monitor with a camera was on top of the desk. Some clothes and toiletries were on the bed. The room smelled of disinfectant, and Avi could hear a slight hum from electrical equipment. The man said, "Please relax. Everything will become clear soon."

As she looked at the desk, she saw a stack of books for her current classes. The clothes were her size. The shampoo, toothpaste, and other toiletries were all the brands she used. As she digested what this meant, a chime sounded, and the computer monitor turned on. She could see the outline of a man but not his face.

"Welcome, Avi. You may refer to me as Seven. First, my apologies regarding the nature of your visit, or for that matter, not being able to meet face-to-face."

Avi looked into the camera. "I was abducted, and I understand why I can't see you. Let's get to the point. What do you want?"

"Excellent! No silly banter necessary. We represent an organization we'll refer to as the Faction. We are interested in the technology your mother and Professor Anderson are developing. We're very intrigued by the possibilities and want to push the concept to much greater levels. Your parents were aware of our interest, but they were reluctant to work with us. We felt you and Noah could help us persuade them to change their minds."

"You mean you planned to take us hostage, which would force them to work with you."

"Not exactly. All we need is access to the work they've completed so far. We plan to extend that work with our scientists who are not as 'constrained' as your parents. Our belief is many parties could and should benefit from this work, not just your selfish government."

"So, if they turn over their research, you'll send me back?"

"Exactly! Tomorrow we will reach out to your mother and Professor Anderson, and this will all be worked out. I'm sorry Noah could not join you, as we felt this would make your stay much more agreeable. For now, please rest. We'll wake you in the morning."

Home

Back at the Verma house, the three scientists discussed the night's events and what to do next.

"Jens, who do you think would do this?" implored Indira, wringing her hands.

"This seems too extreme to be the typical protestors, and I see no other motive for trying to take both children other than to gain access to our research."

Kellen looked at him, "Who would go to these extremes?"

Jens' brow furrowed. "I have a suspicion."

Indira agreed. "No one else knows about our work. We need to tell him."

Jens confided to Kellen, "Based on tonight's events, you need to know. Soon after Ajax was born and his training program had begun, we discovered a leak inside one of our funding agencies. Since only a few people had access to our large mammal program, we knew it had to be one of them. Our DOD contacts were able to trace the leak back to an NSF Director who was having an affair. The woman he was involved with turned out to be an industrial spy. She sold information she obtained to various corporate bidders. Our program was a bit of a conundrum for her. After making a couple of inquiries, a group calling themselves the Faction contacted her. As far as we can tell, she met with them and was never heard from again."

Kellen looked at Indira and raised his eyebrows. She shook her head. "It's all very mysterious. We don't know if she took the money and went elsewhere, or if they eliminated her. Either way, she couldn't be found."

Jens continued, "Shortly afterwards, they reached out to us. When we rejected their overtures, they made it clear they would obtain our research one way or another. The lab was broken into twice, and the second time they took Ajax. We haven't heard from them since, so we thought they were satisfied and would not bother us again."

Kellen shook his head, "Why wasn't I told? I thought the break-ins were related to protesters. Do you think Ajax is still out there?" Then he said, "Never mind, what do we do now?"

Jens said simply, "We wait."

The Warehouse

Sleep had not come easy for Avi, so the alarm clock's chime was initially confusing. She struggled to determine where she was and what she was hearing. As the lights in the room slowly came on, Avi heard soft noises that sounded like a mountain stream. After a few moments, a voice said, "Avi, please wake up now. Someone will stop by to escort you to the shower shortly." After her long night, she was looking forward to the warm water. She gathered her toiletries and fresh clothes and waited.

After a few minutes, she heard a light knock on the door, followed by the sharp click of the lock. One of the four abductors waited for her outside. As she walked by the door with the black circle, she noticed it was half-open, and she saw a large black dog inside watching. Remembering her conversation with Kellen, she attempted to make the sign she had seen Noah use to greet Sasha. She tried to hide her surprise when she saw his ear rotate slightly in response. Forcing herself to look away, she was stunned by the realization Ajax was onsite.

As the warm water from the shower rushed over her, she contemplated what seeing Ajax meant. He didn't seem to be a prisoner, but why was he here? Going through the motions of drying her hair and brushing her teeth, she debated whether or not to try to communicate with him.   After running through the possibilities, she decided there was little to lose.

Thanking the gods that she had occasionally helped Noah practice his signs with Sasha, she picked one that no one but Ajax would notice. She also hoped he knew these signs since she had no idea how far his training had progressed with Kellen. As she walked by the open door, she signed, "Talk?" His response was an immediate yes.

"Oh, WOW! A dog! May I pet him? It's so lonely and scary here!"

Her captor's first response was, "No, let's go." But she turned on her young girl charm, and after a big-eyed "PLEASE," he said, "Fine, pet the dog while I get your breakfast. But the cameras are watching, so don't try anything."

Avi's signing ability was limited compared to Kellen's or Noah's, so it would be easier and faster if she could talk to him. Moving closer, she said loudly, "What a beautiful dog. Can I pet you?" As she ruffled his soft fur, she whispered out of the camera's view, "Hi, Ajax. I'm Avika. I'm so happy to meet you. Sorry about the hug. I'm guessing you aren't a fan of affection."   The turn of his head signed indifference. She realized his communication skills weren't as honed as Sasha's.

"Are you a captive?" Another turned head. After a moment, she realized what he might be communicating.

"Is it complicated?"

"Yes."

"Who are these people?" She inwardly groaned at the foolishness of the question, but his response was emphatic and straightforward.

"BAD."

"Will you help me?" He answered, "Yes," and then her captor returned.

"Enough playing with the dog! Go eat your breakfast in your room."

She looked back at Ajax as she left the room. She marveled how, like Sasha, his bearing was proud, strong, and he seemed to see right through a person. Avi felt a mixture of relief to see him combined with confusion as to why he stayed with these people.

The Center

The email came to Professor Verma early the next morning.

Professors,
As you know, we have Avika. We mean her no harm and will gladly trade her for what we need. Our demands are simple:

- Provide your primary research documentation on the Protectors for the last five years.
- Provide access to the training programs Dr. Jackson has developed.

- Do not contact the authorities regarding this e-mail.
- Maintain this silence in the future and continue to share your work.

At precisely 11:00 AM, use the link below to see and communicate with Avika.

She shared a printed copy with Jens and Kellen in the conference room. She looked at Jens, "Do you think they know about Sasha?" Before he could answer, their assistant, Sarah, knocked on the door.

"Excuse me. There's a Sergeant Murphy here to see you."

Professor Verma requested, "Please send her in."

Sergeant Murphy entered, and seeing the look of dejection in the room, said, "One small piece of good news. The AMBER alert had some success. We have two confirmed sightings of a van heading north on Route 95 that match Noah's description. The timing fits. We also have a picture from a traffic camera that provides more detail on the license plate. The van was rented several days ago and has yet to be turned in. The information on the rental agreement is likely falsified, but we'll have it shortly."

The Sergeant paused for effect, "But the real question is, have they contacted you yet?"

Avi's mom frowned, "Not yet.   Is that unusual?"

The Sergeant shrugged. "To be honest, I'm not sure when they'll contact you, but I'm confident they will. Let me know the moment you hear anything."

The Warehouse

As Avi ate her meager breakfast at the desk, the chime sounded, and the screen turned on.

"Good morning, Avi. I trust you slept well. I also heard you met Ajax this morning. As I'm sure your mother has told you, he is an exceptional canine. We're working with him to understand the depths of his capabilities and have concluded he has amazing intelligence."

Avi thought to herself, *But Mr. Seven, you haven't figured out he can communicate.*

Seven's voice continued, "We only want to harness and share those amazing capabilities. Capabilities your government would like to utilize for less than humanitarian purposes. But enough about that. Your mother has received an e-mail stating you will speak to her this morning at 11:00, precisely 90 minutes from now. We would like you ready at that time."

Avi rolled her eyes. "I was thinking about going to the mall later this morning. Not sure I can fit it in."

"Ah, there's that exquisite sense of humor. Please keep it up. We want it to be clear to her and Professor Anderson you are being treated well, and everyone simply wants this to be resolved. Please keep your communication to those two topics. Attempt anything else, and we will terminate the call immediately."

Avi responded, "I understand. Meanwhile, may I visit with Ajax again? Being with him helps keep me calm."

Seven replied, "Ajax is in training this morning. I'll patch in the feed of his session on your screen before the meeting with your mother. I see no reason you can't meet with Ajax over lunch."

Avi said, "I really appreciate it. You don't know what it means to me."

"Here is the live feed. I'll set an alarm to notify you 15 minutes prior to the meeting with your mother."

The light on the camera went out, and the screen switched to show Ajax and his trainers. Avi once again admired how majestic he looked. He was slightly larger than Sasha but had the same deep brown eyes, alert ears, and confident stance. The training session started with him responding to a set of commands any well-trained dog might know. Avi smiled, thinking how Ajax must feel being subject to such simple activities. She watched as he progressed to working through complicated mazes and puzzles and responding to various scenarios typical dogs wouldn't be able to address.

As she watched, she sensed he was holding back in many circumstances. He didn't want his trainers to realize the extent of his capabilities. Once again, she wondered what his end game might be.

An hour sped by, and she realized it was time to prepare for the call. She thought through the key messages she wanted to communicate:

- 45 miles
- Warehouse
- Near highway
- Ajax here

The Center

After much debate, the group decided only Professors Anderson and Verma would be on the video call from her office. The image and audio would be duplicated on the monitor in the conference room where Kellen, Sasha, and Noah would watch. This group would focus on identifying hidden messages Avi might try to send. Sasha, in particular, was to be on alert for any signs indicating Avi felt immediate danger.

At precisely 11:00, the professors clicked on the link initiating the conference call. They signed in, and the session started. Initially, the camera on the other side did not activate. A male voice came over the speakers, "Good morning, professors. Thank you for joining us. You may refer to me as Seven. I will keep this preamble brief, as I know you want to see Avika. Our request is simple. You know what we want. Meet our demands, and we will return her. Is that clear?"

Professor Verma's voice was flat. "Crystal. Now may I see my daughter?"

Avi's image appeared on the screen. Seeing her distraught mother, she gasped and said, "MOM!" Then steeling herself, she regained control and said, "I'm so happy to see you." Her hands seemed a bit fidgety as she stated, "Don't worry, they're treating me well. I just hope you can resolve all of this soon."

Her mom responded softly, "We'll do anything and everything we can to get this resolved. I miss you."

Seven's voice returned. "This all sounds very promising. Please say your goodbyes, and we will start working on the details."

Avi waved at the camera, "I'll see you soon. I know it."

Her mom returned the wave as the image blinked off. Seven stated, "You have 24 hours to develop a plan that satisfies our request. We will send you another link to speak at that time."

"Will I be able to speak to my daughter?"

"Of course. Now I suggest you get to work."

Shutting down her computer completely, Professor Verma shook her head, "Totally predictable but still unnerving. Let's find out what they learned."

In the conference room, they found Kellen and Noah in a disagreement. On the whiteboard, Kellen had written:

45 → miles, min, other
Highway → near, hear, both
Storage → shed, building, warehouse
Dog → Sasha, Ajax, unknown

Kellen was saying, "To me, it seemed like the 45 refers to minutes. Her hand sign was not clear."

Noah shook his head. "I know Avi. She would try to let us know how far they traveled. Sasha, you caught the reference first. What do you think?"

Kellen and Noah watched her carefully. Kellen replied, "Fine, let's start with miles. And I think we all agree she was trying to tell us they were near the highway." Sasha and Noah both nodded.

Noah went to the third note. "I think a shed is not large enough to have the facility we saw. Agreed?" He looked to Sasha, who signaled agreement. Noah added, "You're right. If she had been more elaborate on this sign, she would have risked detection. Let's hold on to that one and see what comes up as possible locations."

Looking over at the two professors, Kellen started to summarize. "Avi's signing was rough since she hasn't practiced much, and she had to make it look like she was just nervously moving her hands."

Professor Verma interrupted, "Do you think they knew she was communicating?"

Noah interjected, "Unlikely, even Kellen and I didn't know what she was doing right away. Sasha caught the '45' and 'dog' on the first pass. We had to re-watch to identify the rest. She mixed in a lot of noise, and no one outside this room knows the language."

Kellen looked down. "Well, that's not entirely true. The one other individual who knows this language is Ajax. I developed it to communicate with him. It has changed some, but he could have detected her message. That's what worries me about the last message. I think she's saying Ajax may be there. This news is concerning. If Ajax has turned against us, he could realize she's attempting to send a message."

Noah's dad looked around the room. "So, in summary, the location is about 45 miles away, near a highway, in a large storage facility or warehouse."

He projected a large map of the area onto the screen. He had previously placed markers at each location the Amber Alert had resulted in a sighting. "Based on our knowledge of the truck's direction and the distance, the likely destination is in this area." He circled a three-mile section of the highway. "Using a composite satellite and map view, we can narrow it down to buildings here and here which match the criteria."

The satellite view zoomed in on the first potential location, which appeared to be an Amazon distribution center based on its layout. Noah shook his head. "Do we agree there is too much activity around there for this to be the site?" Nods all around as the second location came into focus.

Professor Anderson continued, "This appears to be a site that was formerly a sawmill. For the most part, it appears abandoned. However, this set of buildings right here seems to be maintained. They are not visible from the road, and they back to this large wooded area by the river."

He looked over and said, "Indira, this is ultimately your decision. We can alert the authorities, but I am not sure they are to be trusted. We can turn the research over, but I think this could have much greater ramifications. Or, we can attempt to extract her ourselves, but we don't have the expertise to do it."

Kellen cleared his throat. "I think the big wild card is Ajax. If he's on our side, we might be able to get her out. Otherwise, that option seems crazy."

Avi's mom frowned. "I think we should consider our emergency plan."

Kellen said, "The 'False Research' Plan?"

"Yes, we've spent considerable time preparing two sets of notebooks. One set contains the real research, and the other set, we've intentionally falsified. We also have duplicate reports we developed for just such an eventuality. Everything is close enough to look credible and will appear to be useful."

Noah's dad agreed. "I concur. Let us proceed."

The Warehouse

After the call ended, Avi tried to maintain her composure while emotionally she felt like breaking down in tears. Seeing the light on the camera, she said out loud, "Was that acceptable?"

Seven replied, "It was fine, Avi. We are happy with the outcome and will have you speak to them again tomorrow. Meanwhile, would you like to join Ajax for lunch? He's taking a break from his training and is available. Although I must warn you, he doesn't tend to enjoy company."

The captor who had brought her breakfast knocked on the door, and after a moment, entered. "It's time for your lunch. I've been told you want to eat with the dog. Not sure why you'd like to do that, but I'll bring you to him."

As they walked through the halls, Avi noticed a couple of unmarked doorways. She assumed they were offices for the trainers and her captors. She suspected not many of them stayed here overnight. They went through the door at the end of the hall. A warehouse had been transformed into the training area where she had seen Ajax.

Ajax was looking at a bowl of kibble on the ground but hadn't started eating. Next to him was a small table with a bag from a fast-food restaurant.

The man said, "I hope you like burgers. You have forty minutes before training resumes." He turned and walked away.

Remembering Ajax's training session, Avi realized multiple cameras could see her. Turning on the "little girl" act, she said in a loud voice, "Hi, Handsome Boy! I bet you're hungry after all that exercise." She bent down and picked up his bowl, putting it on the seat next to her. "Is that better?"

He signed, "Thank you." Then, after a moment, he signed, "Careful."

Rubbing her face in the thick fur on the back of his neck, she whispered, "Sorry for the food, the affection, everything."

"Okay." Then he put together three more words, "Happy," "See," "You."

She involuntarily squeezed him and felt him push his head against her. Into his fur, she whispered, "Is it easier for me to ask questions and have you respond?"

"Yes."

In a normal voice, she said, "You were a good boy this morning!" Scratching behind his ears, she kept up the exuberant girl shtick. "You're *sooo* smart and strong!"

She took a bite of her burger and let out an involuntary, "Yuck!" It probably hadn't been good to start with, and now that it was cold, it was pretty disgusting. She watched him pick at his kibble.

To keep up appearances, she ate and chatted away at some nonsense in a voice easily heard. Then, as she bent down to give Ajax a bite of her burger, which he refused, she whispered, "Can you help me escape?"

"Yes."

"Tonight?"

"No."

"Tomorrow?"

"Yes."

He signaled the number "8" and then a "2."

"8:00 at night? Because there are only two guards?"

"Yes."

She continued her chatter, then whispered one more, "Sorry for all of this," apology as she pushed her face into his soft fur.

He seemed to shrug and responded, "Like" and then "You."

The guard came and took her back to her room. As she walked away, she felt Ajax watching her. She turned and winked at him. To her surprise, he blinked his eyes in response.

The Center

The scientists were diligently working to put the finishing touches on the falsified notebooks and reports. They believed they could provide a credible-looking body of research within the next two days in exchange for getting Avi back.

After several discussions, they still could not determine how to complete the transfer. They debated providing only part of the data set or having some way of corrupting it if Avi was not returned. Ultimately, they agreed the only option that would not place Avi at risk was to turn over all of the (falsified) research and hope the Faction's leaders would release her.

The email with the new link came late that evening.

Professors,

We hope you are making progress toward fulfilling our arrangement. Our next scheduled meeting is tomorrow at 11:00 AM. Use the link below to see and communicate with Avika and provide us with your plan's details.

The night and following morning dragged by, despite the ongoing efforts to organize the data.   Finally, 11:00 arrived, and they initiated the video conference. After signing in, they heard Seven say, "Good morning, Professors.   I trust you have been working diligently on a plan."

Avi's mom took the lead. "We have. We have been organizing all of the data and reports into a digital package, which will be ready in 24 hours. When you return Avi tomorrow, we will provide the details on how to access the data."

"This is not acceptable. When you provide access to the data, and we confirm the validity, we will release Avi. Our only goal is the data. It's gold to us."

"How do we know you'll..."

"YOU DON'T!"

The sudden outburst from Seven surprised everyone.

"We are in charge here, the Alpha, as it were. We tire of you and your silly games. We have no desire to keep the girl any longer than necessary. Nor do we intend to hurt her. It's simple. Provide us access. We give you the girl. We will send you the link to upload your research. Now, do you agree? Do you want to see her?"

Professor Verma stated, "We agree. And, of course, we want to see her."

Avi appeared on the monitor, her voice tentative, "Hi Guys. Everything okay?" Like the day before, she fidgeted and seemed nervous.

Her mom nodded. "It's all set. We'll have everything ready tomorrow."

"Awesome. I can't wait to get home. But you'll never guess who I've been visiting with!" Per an arrangement with her captors, she had Ajax join her on camera. "I'm sure you know who this is."

As Ajax looked into the camera, Avi's mom gasped, and she heard Jens utter a soft "Oh my" under his breath. She could only imagine the response in the other room.

"Guys, he's doing great here. They treat him really well, and his training regimen is amazing." Ajax showed no emotion but continued to look into the camera intently. His ears moved slightly, but otherwise; he could have been made of stone.

Seven's voice came on. "Okay, enough. When the information is downloaded tomorrow, we will provide instructions on how to find Avi." The link was broken.

Indira looked at Jens, "Can you believe that?"

He frowned, "We always assumed Ajax was there. I guess we shouldn't be surprised."

They walked into the conference room. Kellen's notes were scribbled on the whiteboard:

- 8:00 tonight → what?

- 2 guards → Fewer guards in the evening?
- Ajax

Noah looked at his dad. "Wow! Ajax is really there, and it appears he's working with them." Glancing at Sasha, he asked, "Are you sure?" Even to those who couldn't read signs, her exasperation came through.

Noah explained, "Sasha says he's not working for them. She senses his loyalty is to Avi."

Kellen interjected, "I didn't see Avi communicate anything like that."

Noah shook his head. "She didn't. Sasha sees it in Ajax's body language. If I interpret this correctly, the facility is lightly guarded at night. Ajax is going to help her escape because they don't intend to let her go."

Professor Anderson ran his hand over his chin. "We cannot ignore this possibility. I recommend we get in a position to assist if they attempt to escape. We will continue to prepare the data package in the event our hypothesis is incorrect. Agreed?"

Everyone looked at Indira. She flatly replied, "I think it's the only logical choice."

The Warehouse

Avi spent the afternoon thinking about Ajax and the impending attempt to escape. She tried to nap to conserve energy, but she was a bundle of nerves. When dinner finally came, it was cold fried chicken, which did little to satisfy her hunger or settle her stomach. Watching the clock crawl towards 8:00 PM, she was startled at 7:55 when alarms suddenly blared throughout the building. A sprinkler showered her room with water, and she heard the lock on her door click.

Opening the door revealed a world gone mad. Sprinklers were drenching the hallway while alarms blared and an emergency light flickered on and off. The most surprising thing Avi saw was her cell phone, lying outside the door in a Ziploc® bag. Quickly unlocking it, she sent a quick text to her mother:

A: Escaping

She turned to the exit door when Ajax appeared from the opposite direction. He signaled what she believed meant "Follow." Inexplicably, he ran further into the facility. A guard appeared from his door and cursed loudly, "What the f*$%?"

Seeing the guard, Ajax turned, and to her shock, growled at Avi. He then made the "Follow" sign and continued running further into the facility. As she chased after him, she heard the guard yelling into his radio, "SHE'S TRYING TO GET THE DOG! SHE'S CHASING HIM INTO THE TRAINING AREA. STAY BY THE DOOR!"

She heard the guard behind her, and glancing back, saw him grab something from his waist. As Ajax rounded a corner, she saw the guard preparing to throw what appeared to be bolas, a tripping weapon, at her. Ducking into an open side door, she heard it clatter by on the floor. Sprinting away, she managed to stay ahead of him as he slipped on the wet floor.

Following Ajax to the training area, she went through a door that entered a short hallway and then through a second door just as the guard entered. Ajax had stopped and was looking at a large red button labeled ISOLATION. She instinctively hit the button and heard a loud snap. As the guard ran into the now-locked door, his face slammed into the window, leaving a sizeable bloody mark. She saw him slide to the floor as Ajax grabbed her sleeve.

Following him through the darkened training area, Avi marveled at Ajax's abilities. She could still hear the alarms in the other area of the building. Whispering, she asked, "Did you do that?"

His look provided the answer. Impatiently, he continued into the building.

Avi realized Ajax was picking a route to prevent detection by any cameras as they slipped through the obstacles. The off-site captors were undoubtedly trying to figure out what was going on and had likely heard the guard's communication. They made it to a door on the far side of the facility, only to find it locked.

Ajax turned to one of the obstacles she had seen him navigate during his training. It involved jumping up onto a series of platforms that were each several feet higher than the prior and quite far apart. As Avi watched, he quickly made his way up, but on the next-to-last platform, he seemed to jump right into the wall. Avi gasped as he disappeared. Soon his face reappeared in an opening near the top of the wall. Realizing she could never follow, Avi breathed a sigh of relief when he pushed a rope ladder over the edge.

After quickly ascending the ladder and crawling over the top, she realized she was on a walkway that provided access to the offices' utilities inside the warehouse. As she stepped forward, she felt Ajax bite her shirt, pulling her back and preventing her from falling off. Heart pounding, she realized there was no handrail, and the walkway wound its way over the top of the offices.

Ajax stood close, and she placed her hand on his back as he slowly helped them negotiate their way over the offices. When they finally reached the outside wall, Avi felt a small door. Slowly opening it, she could see the second guard in the parking lot directly below them. He was agitated and seemed to be looking in every direction, except up.

Next to her, she felt Ajax tense. Carefully calculating the distance, he jumped so that his full weight hit the man's back, throwing him forward. The guard's head slapped the ground, and a pool of blood formed below it.

Feeling queasy from the sight, Avi suddenly saw the main door to her right start to open. As the other guard started to step out, a blur of white suddenly slammed into him. He exclaimed, "WHAT THE F$%#," as he scrambled back into the building.

She saw Kellen emerge from the shadows and look up at her. "Just step off and lift your legs. I'll catch you; I promise!" Relieved to see him, she did as he instructed. Once she was down safely, Kellen looked at Sasha peering through the half-open door. "Is he there?" She signaled, "No."

Reaching down, he felt the fallen man's neck. He was alive. A quick search revealed the guard's phone. Kellen used its emergency feature and placed a 911 call. "Help! I'm at the old sawmill on Sycamore Street. My partner has fallen and hit his head. HURRY! IT'S BAD!" As the operator asked for more information, he ended the call and wiped the phone with the man's shirt.

Kellen looked at Avi and the two dogs. "He'll live, I think. It's time for us to go. No telling who'll get here first." As they started to walk away, he noticed Ajax was standing still. Looking at Sasha, Kellen gritted his teeth. "What do you mean, he has unfinished business?" Turning to Ajax, he implored,

"Please!?"   Ajax turned and walked back toward the guard.

Home

As the van pulled into the Anderson's driveway, the two professors and Noah came rushing out. Kellen's last text had simply said, "Success," and they were desperate for the details. The doors opened, and they watched Kellen, Avi, and Sasha wearily climb out. Avi immediately ran into her mother's arms and started to cry.

Noah asked, "What's wrong? Where's Ajax?"

Kellen shook his head, and they all went quiet when a police cruiser came to a screeching halt in front of the house. Sergeant Murphy and Officer Janes jumped out. Momentary relief showed on Murphy's face, which was replaced with anger, as she turned to Avi's mom.

"What happened?"

Noah's dad started to answer, and Murphy snapped, "Her! I asked her."

Indira looked into Murphy's eyes and said in a smooth, steady voice. "Approximately 70 minutes ago, we received a text from Avi indicating she was escaping. We tracked her cellphone to a location just off Exit 54." Looking at Janes, she continued, "We didn't trust the authorities not to leak the information."

Janes shook his head. "A 911 call was received near that location indicating someone was hurt. But when the local authorities arrived, there was nothing to be found. However, it does appear someone has been using the site recently."

Murphy glared at Janes, then turning to Avi, she asked, "What happened? We'll want a full statement at the station, but what do you know that can help us find your abductors right now?"

Avi looked at her mother and Noah's father, and, remembering their earlier warning, she chose her words carefully. "As you said, I'll provide a complete account later. But the short version is I was kidnapped by people who want information from Professor Anderson. I don't know everything, but they are running some kind of training facility. There was a dog there, and I think they want access to the advanced training research being done at the Center."

Her voice cracking, she said, "They treated me well, but I was pretty scared. Tonight, there was some kind of malfunction, and the whole place seemed to go nuts. Alarms were blaring, sprinklers spraying, you name it. My door unlocked, and I got out. I found my cellphone and managed to send a quick text before a guard started chasing me. I got away and found a way out, but doing so, I fell on the other guard from a second-story door. I think his head got hurt pretty bad."

Janes stepped forward and touched Avi's shoulder. The deep-throated growl from Sasha made him pull his hand back. Murphy shoved Janes from behind and said, "Stay away from her!" Speaking directly to Avi, she said, "We need you to come down and provide a statement. We have to find these people."

Just then, a black Suburban pulled up. Two men in dark suits stepped out. The passenger stated, "We're from the Department of Defense's Research Intelligence Agency, the DRIA. We'll take over from here." Glaring at Professor Anderson, he said through gritted teeth, "Why. Were. We. Not. Notified."

Professor Anderson held his gaze and replied evenly, "Because we did not trust you would be sufficiently careful."

The DRIA agent said to the police officers, "You can go now. This is our investigation from now on." The other agent caught Janes' eye as he left. Sasha watched the two carefully.

Returning his attention to the group, the lead agent introduced himself and his colleague, "I'm Director Michael Johnston in charge of the Special Projects group. This is my colleague, Agent David Williams. Our role is to monitor any threats against the projects we sponsor. The DOD is one of two agencies supporting the Protectors program, and, as you know, we're supposed to be notified if there's a possible security risk."

The last words were aimed at Professor Anderson, who seemed unfazed by them. In a calm, even tone, he responded, "Abduction of one of our children hardly qualifies as a Department of Defense concern. We had no way of knowing this was related to the program."

Johnston interrupted, "Our intelligence indicates it was directly targeting the Protectors. We need to speak to Avika. We want the real story, not the half-truth you've concocted for the police."

Professor Anderson glanced at Noah and Sasha before saying, "You realize with one call I can have you taken off this case? But I agree Avi should speak to you," glancing at Agent Williams and then back to Johnston, "and only you. And, naturally, her mother will be present."

As Williams tried to protest, Johnston said, "Agreed. Williams, go get us coffee. It'll be a long night, so get a lot and don't hurry back."

Williams shot daggers at the professor but reluctantly went over to the Suburban. Revving it loudly, he drove off into the night.

Johnston's face softened as he looked at Avi and said, "Let's go inside. I need you to tell me everything. Don't worry. You won't get in trouble." Glancing at the two parents, he confessed, "I admit I would have done the same for my daughter."

Inside the house, Noah, Kellen, Sasha, and Professor Anderson waited while Avi recounted her tale in the other room. Once they were alone, Noah blurted out, "Where's Ajax!?"

Kellen looked down. "I don't know. He refused to come with us. Sasha indicated he had unfinished business." Looking at her, he raised his eyebrows, "Do you know anything else?" Shaking his head at her reply, he added, "He looked healthy, and he is clearly on top of his game. The way he took out the one guard was unbelievable."

Noah spoke quietly, "I think I understand his motive. I'm guessing he's the only one who has ever penetrated the Faction. We only see a tiny piece of what they are and don't understand their broader objective. He feels these are bad people. They believe he's just a smart dog who doesn't understand anything. He probably knows more about them than all of the intelligence agencies in the world combined. I think he wants to take them down."

Looking at Sasha, he said, "We have a more immediate problem, don't we?"

Interpreting for Sasha, Kellen announced, "Officer Janes and Agent Williams both have bad intent. Further, they know each other." He paused and spoke directly to Sasha, "How do you know? But couldn't the look have been a coincidence? Oh boy, alright." Shaking his head, he continued, "She's adamant. They are conspiring against us. She doesn't know who they work for, but they've penetrated local law enforcement and the DRIA, so it's pretty pervasive."

Professor Anderson asked, "So what do they plan to do?"

Noah took the lead. "I think they're going to break into the lab again. They were hoping you would hand over the research and help them 'easy-peasy,' but they knew all along it would take more to get full cooperation. I recommend we put all of the false data in place so they find it when they come back. We also need to prepare an exit strategy."

His father replied, "I concur. The DRIA will want to inspect the labs first thing tomorrow. Let's start replacing the data immediately afterwards. Kellen, how long to modify your area?"

Raising his eyebrows, Kellen speculated, "Two days or so? The false data already exists, but archiving and removing the real data will take time."

"Two days is too long. I will take Noah out of school to help. We need to discuss all of this with Indira and Avi."

As he came out of the other room, Officer Johnston was saying, "Great start. We'll finish in the morning after the tour of the lab. I don't think either Avika or Noah should go to school tomorrow."

Speaking into his phone, he said, "Geez, Williams, where are you? Get over here now." Waving, he walked out the door.

The Center

Noah, Avi, and Sasha all got the day off from school. Since the DRIA had suppressed any local publicity of the abduction, their parents had to provide some flimsy excuse. In reality, all three of them were outstanding students working in programs with no hard deadlines.

Sasha, Noah, and Kellen waited in the lab while Avi and the two professors spoke to Director Johnston. Kellen asked if they wanted to practice or do some scenarios, but no one's heart was in it. Finally, Noah asked, "What's Ajax's story?" Kellen got up and closed the door. Sasha trotted over to join them since she knew little of his background and was just a puppy when he was abducted.

"Well, as you know, the Animal Intelligence Initiative has been in place for slightly over ten years. Most of the original work focused on small mammals, such as mice and gerbils. The two-pronged approach of genetic modification and training resulted in interesting outcomes, but they were mostly academic. I mean, what practical purpose is it to determine how fast a mouse can navigate a maze, or if it can differentiate between paths, one of which leads to a preferred cheese?"

Smiling, Kellen looked at Sasha and continued, "The real change was when your parents proposed developing more intelligent service animals. When I joined the program, the first attempts were canines with above-average intelligence, mostly due to selective breeding and minor genetic modifications. These animals were fun to train and develop, but really, they were just outstanding examples of the breed. We considered them 'safe to release,' and we placed them in homes."

Kellen continued, "The DOD met with us and asked if we could push the technology further. Much further. We proposed the Protectors program, and the first success was Ajax. Although he looked like a typical black German Shepherd, we knew he was special, even as a puppy. I had to create new languages to communicate with him. It was reality-altering. He could do things I hadn't imagined. I started to develop new tests to determine the extent of his intuition. The combination of canine instincts and sensory capabilities with near, and in some cases beyond, human intelligence made him seem clairvoyant at times. The intent was to create 'super companions' who would provide protection in ways no other bodyguard could. Ajax turned out to be so much more."

Kellen sighed. "But his rapid progress was raising issues and expectations we hadn't anticipated. I've recently learned there was a leak at the DOD. Our lab was broken into, and afterward, they wanted to take Ajax away. Of course, we refused. Meanwhile, we had a second success when Sasha was born soon after Ajax turned two. To protect her, we engaged in the hide-in-plain-sight approach. We told the DOD and NSF we wanted to see if a non-genetically modified dog could achieve similar success to Ajax."

"Even though she exceeds Ajax in many capabilities..." looking over at Sasha, he added, "You should blush," he continued, "we've always kept the extent of her intelligence a secret. All of the reports to the funding agencies have provided limited insight."

Kellen explained, "Ajax and Sasha were together for a few months, which I believe contributed to her rapid learning ramp. After we lost him, I almost gave up." Following a moment of silence, he smiled wistfully at Sasha and asked, "But how could I let you down?"

The door opened, and Avi joined them. "Jeez, I feel like a cheese sandwich that's been burnt to a crisp."

Kellen empathized, "I was only at the warehouse for the last few minutes, and Johnston talked to me for an hour. Did you tell him everything?"

Avi rolled her eyes. "Everything. He made me tell him every detail about Ajax. I think they are frustrated we didn't get him back. He thinks Ajax has 'turned.' His words. I asked him, 'Why did he help me get free?' He didn't have a good answer. I also told him off the record to watch his back around Agent

Williams. I've been doing some research on that guy."

Handing them a printout of an unusual tattoo with the numbers 1 and 18, Avi went to the computer and pulled up a website. "This tattoo is common among a group of individuals associated with Separatists in the Pacific Northwest. It's barely visible on his neck, and finding a reference to it online was nearly impossible. Officer Janes has similar ink more prominently displayed on his wrist. My guess is they know each other, and they have an agenda."

Kellen chimed in. "I've been looking into Officer Janes. He's not permanent here. He's on a temporary assignment until Murphy's regular partner returns to active duty. Her partner was mysteriously shot last month. Something is fishy here. Let's tell your parents. Meanwhile, did the DRIA leave?"

Avi nodded.

"Good. Then it's time to start the data swap," Kellen announced.

An Undisclosed Location

Seven's weekly update with the Chairman was going to be unpleasant. The Chairman, who was the founder of the Faction, was known to be a highly placed public official. While Seven had never directly spoken to or seen the man, he dreaded reporting the current situation. Failure, as he knew, tended to have dramatic and sometimes fatal consequences.

Seven clicked the link, and the session started.

Chairman: Report.

Seven: As you know, we were only able to capture one of the two children.

Chairman: Yes, once again, the boy eluded your ham-fisted attempts to take him.

Seven: In both cases, the assets utilized were based on Central's recommendation. The two men in the alley were from the Separatist group whose goals roughly align with ours. In retrospect, we may have done better to utilize higher-skilled assets, but we erred on the side of confidentiality. This group is extremely secretive. Further, they have additional assets who are well placed to continue support of our efforts.

Chairman: What about the second case?

Seven: We used known members of an Eastern European gang. They have always delivered in the past. They missed the boy but delivered the girl.

Chairman: In both cases, the boy was with the white dog, and it helped him escape. Do we know anything about it?

Seven: In the reports our agent has provided, it appears to be a well-bred dog that has undergone extensive training. It's always with the boy or the researcher, Dr. Jackson. We have been informed this dog is not exceptional like Ajax.

Chairman: Can we be sure?

Seven: We cannot, but if it is, these facts have been very carefully hidden, even from the funding agencies.

Chairman: Let's return to the girl. She was brought to our training area. What happened?

Seven: We detained her and used her as leverage to obtain cooperation from the professors. It appeared to be on track, but a malfunction in the laboratory allowed her to escape.

Chairman: A malfunction?

Seven: I'm investigating. The fire alarm was activated, but my operatives have not been able to ascertain how. It turns out the door locks deactivate in the event of a fire.

The facility was not created to be a holding area. I've considered an accidental triggering by one of the guards, but this does not seem to be the case. It is also possible, but unlikely, the girl, or someone from the outside, triggered it.

Chairman: Did the girl learn Ajax was at the facility?

Seven: We deliberately allowed her to have contact. Our expectation was she would bond and see he is happy with his situation, which would help convince her mother to cooperate.

Chairman: But she got away?

Seven: She did. It was a misjudgment to only have two guards at night. I still find it difficult to believe she managed to accomplish this on her own. Somehow it appears she retrieved her phone and contacted her family. One of the guards saw Dr. Jackson and the white dog meeting her. The guard claims the dog attacked him.

Chairman: And Ajax?

Seven: He appeared to be friendly with the girl but would not go with her when she ran away. The guard saw him attempting to get away from her.

Chairman: Well, with the exception of that fact, this is all extremely disappointing. I trust you have devised the next steps?

Seven: I have. We are continuing to monitor the situation through our assets in the DRIA and local police department. We will infiltrate the lab this weekend and obtain the research documentation. Our intent is to do this without setting off any alarms.

Chairman: Will it be enough to fulfill our plans?

Seven: Unlikely. At some point, we expect to require the assistance of the three researchers. We have concluded they will not cooperate freely, so this will ultimately require an abduction.

Chairman: Why not take them now?

Seven: We are still setting up the facility. It should be ready in several weeks. So far, there have only been minor setbacks. I assure you we will achieve our ultimate goal.

Chairman: Keep me informed.

Seven disconnected the session.

Home Several Days Later

Avi pointed to the photo on the website. "See? There he is right there."

Noah enlarged the picture and shifted it to his large monitor. "You're definitely correct. It's Janes. Nicely done. Who are these guys again?"

"They call themselves 'Separatist Northwest.' They say they are modern-day versions of the Pilgrims. From what I can tell, they aren't really concerned about separating from any church, as much as they want to establish an independent country."

Noah wrinkled his nose at Sasha, who responded in kind. "Like the Plymouth Rock Pilgrims? Why do they want to separate anyway?"

"According to their website, they are concerned about the direction this country is going in and society in general. More specifically, they want to set up a separate country in the remote Pacific Northwest. I think they really want to keep everyone else out."

Sticking his tongue out at Sasha, Noah got a laugh from Avi as they watched Sasha stick out her pink tongue at them. "Seems like everybody wants that these days. So why would they be connected to the Faction?"

Avi shook her head. "I don't know enough about the Faction to hazard a guess. But I do not buy that load of manure of 'they just want to share our parents' technology with the world.'"

Noah's dad knocked on the door. "A break-in is currently taking place at the Center. Noah, please bring the security cameras online."

Noah did as his father requested. The ten cameras appeared as squares on his screen. Nothing seemed to be happening in any of them, typical of a weekend evening. The professor pointed at Camera 4 that showed the reception area. Enlarging it, Noah saw a car pass by the window. His father held up his finger, signaling to wait. About 30 seconds later, the car passed by again.

Professor Anderson explained, "The cameras are on a loop. All of them. That one is the easiest to detect. Bring up the infrared motion detector array."

The array was built on simple infrared motion detection technology like that used to turn on lights. They had installed it without telling anyone, even the DOD. Using detectors that appeared to control the lights, they could see if individuals were moving inside the Center. Viewing the array's output, they could see two intruders in Kellen's laboratory and one in Indira's office.

Noah asked, "Should we call the police?"

Avi shook her head, "I'll bet Officer Janes is waiting for that call. Same with Williams at the DRIA."

Noah's dad pointed out the more important issue. "We want them to succeed. The trick is to make them think they were able to steal the work. That was pretty simple with Kellen's training regimen. It's in a locked cabinet in the laboratory we've made sure they can find. The false training equipment and scenario setups you both helped put in place will reinforce the training guides."

The professor continued, "The harder part is to provide all of the false reports and fake electronic notebooks without it appearing to be a plant. We are hoping they will find my backup drive locked in my office. Once they have it, they will find some very challenging encryption software protecting it."

Avi asked, "What if they don't find it or can't beat it?"

Noah echoed what they were all thinking, "They'll come after us."

The Center

The three men moved like ghosts through the Center. They had disabled the known security measures, which relied on cameras, pressure sensors, and noise detectors, but they were still wary.

Two of them focused on the laboratory and training area. In the training area, they had been instructed to document the layout and equipment used for training. The leader brought out the low-light equipment capable of scanning the area and creating a three-dimensional virtual rendering of the lab. The entire system consisted of several cameras run from an application on the incursion leader's smartphone. Setting the cameras up in the locations prescribed, the leader initiated the scan procedure and went back into the lab.

The second team member had already broken into the locked case that housed what appeared to be logs and manuals. Per their instructions, these were all put inside the waterproof crates they had brought with them. Quickly defeating the simple lock on the desk drawer, the leader packed the very few folders with materials inside them. He doubted there was anything here his employer would find valuable but felt he should be thorough.

The man moved back into the training area; the scan was complete. As he packed up his equipment, the third team member reported in after searching through the female professor's office. Shaking his head to signify he had not found anything significant, he turned to go into the male professor's office.

As the team leader finished packing, he was concerned this was an unsuccessful mission. He doubted anything they were collecting would be considered valuable. Signaling to the other man to move the crates to the van, he went into the hall. The third team member was exiting the office, shaking his head.

Wanting to check for himself, the team leader went into the woman's office. Other than a few pictures of a young girl, the office was pretty Spartan. He checked thoroughly for any secret hiding places. Nothing.

Moving into the man's office, he found pretty much the same. Replace the girl's pictures with a few of a boy and his dog, and it could be the same workspace. He was just about to give up when he decided to take one last look through the small filing cabinet his colleague had already checked. In the back, he noticed extra space that would allow for a hidden compartment. Feeling along the side, he activated a lever that released a door revealing a small safe.

Walking back into the hall, he grabbed the team member's arm who missed the hiding space. As his colleague saw the secret compartment, his eyes got big. The leader pointed to the van to signal he should take the entire cabinet.

Maybe they had found what they were looking for after all.

Home

Noah was watching the output from the array and realized all of the men were in the hall. "I think they are packing up to leave." A minute later and the array stopped detecting any activity. They had noticed the team seemed to search each office multiple times, but there was no way of knowing if the men had found the false data.

His father walked into the room talking on the phone. "Yes, they appear to be done. My guess is if they didn't find it, they will try to break into our homes. I agree. I'd like to go with you and Sasha to assess what happened. We will drop Indira, Avi, and Noah at the restaurant before we visit the Center."

Turning towards Noah and Avi, Jens said, "Please gather your things. I am hoping they found what we left for them. If they didn't, I want us to be away from our homes."

The Center

When Jens, Kellen, and Sasha reached the Center, it was immediately obvious a break-in had occurred. The main door was left open, and the intruders had not attempted to hide the fact the offices had been ransacked. Jens nodded, and Kellen made the 911 call.

"911, may I have your name, location, and the nature of the emergency?"

Kellen stated, "My name is Dr. Kellen Jackson. I'm at the Center for Animal Intelligence Initiative on the university campus.   There's been a break-in at the facility."

"Has anyone been hurt?"

"No."

"Are the intruders still there?"

"We don't know. We just arrived."

"Please move away from the building. I'll dispatch someone right away."

Kellen ended the call and looked over to Jens and Sasha. As she communicated what she found, Kellen provided the translation. "Sasha confirms there were three men. Two of them were also involved in the attempted abduction." He shook his head. "She also says those two have poor hygiene. The third person is new."

Jens looked into his office through the window and said, "The more important point is the file cabinet containing the backup drive is gone. It appears they were able to find it. Let's wait in the parking lot."

After only a few minutes, two officers they didn't know arrived with their lights flashing. As they were getting out of the car, Murphy and Janes pulled in as well. Murphy took charge. Pointing at Janes, she said, "Let's clear the building first. We have no way of knowing if the perpetrators have vacated. Stills, stay with the civilians. Okay, let's go."

Officer Stills stayed back but stepped to the side to communicate with Dispatch. Kellen quietly said to Jens, "Sasha says Janes knows there's no one in the building. He'll report our reactions back to whoever did this."

A few minutes later, the three police officers came out of the building. Murphy announced, "It's clear, but it appears the intruders did quite a bit of damage. We will need you to walk through and identify what they took. We will then close the area off and process the scene."

Janes asserted, "And leave the dog outside. We don't want it contaminating the scene."

Kellen turned to Janes and looked down at him. Janes typically used his physical presence to intimidate people. Except for Murphy, no one in this small town had stood up to him. He wasn't used to facing men who were taller, bigger, and clearly not scared of him. The dog was another thing. Somehow it seemed to see right through him.

Speaking in his low, deep voice, Kellen said, "Sasha works in this lab. She won't be contaminating anything. She goes where we go. You got a problem with that?"

Before he could respond, Murphy stepped between them. "I don't have time for this." Looking at Janes, she asked incredulously, "What's wrong with you?"

During the lab inspection, Kellen pointed out cabinets that the intruders had opened and described the missing manuals and notes. Murphy asked, "Who would be interested in those?"

Kellen shrugged. Knowing Sasha would be watching Janes, he explained, "We consider them confidential, but they would only be useful to someone trying to train service animals. We'll notify our DOD sponsor, but I doubt they'll be too concerned."

The reaction was more significant when they reached Professor Anderson's office. He appeared to be quite shaken when he realized his entire file cabinet was missing. When Murphy asked what was in it, he said primarily written copies of reports, but it was clear he was trying to maintain composure.

Professor Verma's office appeared to be mostly untouched, but Murphy said they would bring her here to confirm nothing was missing.

Back outside, Murphy said they had already checked the video security system and determined someone had shut it down during the robbery. They would process the scene to look for evidence, but she guessed they wouldn't find anything. The perpetrators appeared to be professionals.

Closely watching Jens and Kellen, Murphy asked if they thought this could be connected to the attempts to kidnap the children. Both men shook their heads. Jens added, "No, we have no reason to think so."

Before leaving, she said, "I'll have a detail posted outside your homes for your protection. Please let them know when you come and go."

An Undisclosed Location

Seven had sent a note to the Chairman, knowing he would want an update on the latest developments.

As he clicked the link to start the session, he let out a short sigh.

Chairman: Report.

Seven: The break-in appears to have been successful. We have recovered a backup drive with extremely challenging encryption protection. Our operative reports Professor Anderson was dismayed to find it missing.

Chairman: Was there anything else?

Seven: We found the training regimen for the white dog, Sasha. It was less sophisticated than our current program for Ajax. The dog appears to be unremarkable, but our resource in the local police department believes otherwise. We've instructed him to continue observation but to take no direct action.

Chairman: Keep me informed.

PART 3

The Academy

A month after the break-in, life had returned to its old routines with a few exceptions. Now, an adult and Sasha always had to accompany Noah and Avi when they were off campus grounds. On this clear late autumn morning, the task of walking them to school fell to Kellen. As they walked along the sidewalk, Sasha picked her way around the piles of leaves on the sidewalks while Noah and Avi tended to crash through, enjoying the sound and sensation of the dry leaves.

Avi broke the silence and asked, "Do you think the Academy can win this weekend?" The annual game with their key rival was a few days away, and every year it was a tough battle. The Academy had a small number of students, and even some freshmen like Alex and Will would be playing.

Kellen smiled as he said, "No way. They are up against the most talented quarterback I've seen in a long time. He's even better than his older brothers, who both got scholarships. But go on, I know what you really want to ask."

She looked down. "Do you think everything is okay now?"

Kellen looked at Sasha. "I think everything is fine for now. A lot of your mom's work in the data they stole is real. It's going to take them a long time to figure out what isn't. We also talked directly to the head of the DRIA and told them our suspicions about Williams and Janes. I'm hoping they can start figuring out who these people are, and maybe we can stop them. Meanwhile, we need to stay vigilant."

They reached the Academy gate where Alex, Nico, and Diego were waiting. Kellen stepped over to Alex and gave him a handshake and a half-body "man-hug." "Luck this weekend!"

Alex smiled. "We have more than luck. Noah has reviewed the teams and provided us with a game plan. Even the coach agrees it could work. Personally, I think it's pretty stupid, but I get to be a star. So hey, why not?" He playfully shoved Noah. Sasha had to fight her instinct to nip him in response.

Kellen and Sasha watched them walk across the academy grounds to class. Thinking about the day ahead, Kellen realized he wasn't ready to go to the lab just yet. Plus, he was avoiding any predictable routine. "Trail ride?"

Sasha bounded over and lightly head-butted him. He loved it when she gave in to her joy. He taunted her, "I'm going make you beg me to slow down." Seeing her response, he said, "Yeah, but that was a real technical trail. We're going someplace smooth where I have the advantage." Her nip on the back of his leg caused him to reconsider. "Got it, the Brook. It's kind of in the middle, and we can get there from the Lab."

The Brook Nature Reservation

Kellen was relatively new to riding his bike on trails, and the Brook Reservation was a nice place to learn. The loop was about six miles long with only a few technical spots containing lots of tight twists and turns. It also looped back on itself and, by cutting across, you could walk out to the trailhead in less than a mile if something like a flat tire occurred.

While riding one of the technical sections, Kellen had to get off the bike and walk. Sasha bounded ahead about ten yards and was just turning back when she saw someone in the woods. The person ducked behind a tree. She signaled Kellen that someone was watching them.

When he reached her position, he looked around and said, "Where?" When she indicated the location, they heard crashing as someone attempted to run away through the undergrowth. Dragging the bike through the brush slowed Kellen down. He was finally able to hide it, but then he had to run to catch up to Sasha.

She paused to let him catch his breath and signed it was Officer Janes. Chasing him back toward the entrance, they heard a car starting. "Sasha, we can't catch him."

She turned and started running in the opposite direction. She signaled, "Gate," to him. The Reservation road went around a pond and then passed under the trail before merging onto the highway. There was a gate near the entrance that could be closed that would prevent Janes from accessing the highway.

"Sasha, he saw us communicating. We have to stop him before he gets back into the neighborhood. There's no cell signal in here. We need to make sure he doesn't have a video recording of us that proves you are special. We need his phone."

The two of them sprinted up the trail. They heard a car start in the direction of the trailhead. It was racing toward the entrance when, inexplicably, they heard it slow. A horn blared.

Janes had been following the white dog and Dr. Jackson for weeks. He was sure she was like the dog the Faction was studying, but he could never get proof. He had tried to bug the labs, but the method had failed. When he saw them going out for a bike ride this morning, he hoped this was his chance.

He knew the terrain well from his runs in the Reservation. Once he saw them enter, it was merely a matter of getting in position and taking video of them. He couldn't believe his luck when Kellen stopped for the rocky section and began communicating with the dog. After recording the video, Janes attempted to send it to his contact via text message when he realized two things: There was no signal in the Reservation; and, the dog was watching him.

Knowing he had to get out to the highway to get a cell signal, Janes ran directly toward the trailhead. This meant he cut across the paths, going directly through the woods. The underbrush was thicker than he thought. As he pushed his way through, briars and underbrush raked him. His legs, arms, and face were covered in scratches. But the sacrifice seemed worth it when he made it to the car before his pursuers.

Revving the engine, Janes was elated. He raced down the single-lane entry road. About a half mile before he was out, he saw a pickup truck coming towards him. Blaring his horn, he tried to get the guy to yield. With the patience of Job, the man shook his head and slowly started backing up. He got to a spot where he could pull over enough for the two vehicles to pass. Janes exclaimed "YES" at the top of his lungs as he passed by the truck and drove towards the highway.

Kellen and Sasha's race to close the gate seemed destined for failure until they heard Janes' blaring horn. Pushing himself to the limit, Kellen was on the bridge over the road when he heard Janes' car approaching. As he realized he wouldn't reach the gate in time, he saw Sasha signal "ROCK!"

Picking up a softball-size stone, he wound up and threw it at the lever that controlled the gate's closing mechanism. The rock scored a perfect hit and the gate activated. As it was swinging shut, he was shocked to see Janes veer off the road and attempt to go around the gate. Instead, Janes' car slammed into a tree, deploying the airbags with a bang and shooting up a geyser of hot steam from the smashed radiator.

Carefully maneuvering their way down the hill, Kellen and Sasha arrived almost a full minute after the accident. They could hear a vehicle, likely the one that had blocked Janes earlier, on the road behind them. Cautiously coming around the car's backside, they were surprised to see the rear driver-side door open. The driver's seat looked like a scene from a horror movie with blood and glass everywhere, but it was otherwise empty.

Sasha signaled "Follow," and they ran around the gate, down the single-lane entry road toward the main road beyond. Up ahead, they spotted Janes at the edge of the busy two-lane highway.

He turned to them and was a shock to see. Blood streamed down his face where the glass pieces had embedded after the airbag deployed. It also appeared his nose was broken.

But the big surprise was his expression. He was holding his phone up in triumph, standing with his back to the road. Laughing, he said, "The video just went. We'll see who's the idiot now!" Then, looking at Sasha, he said, "That thing is a monster. You keep it away from me."

Taking an instinctive step backward, he didn't notice the drop-off by the edge of the road. Kellen tried to warn him, but it was too late. As he lost balance, he fell back onto the road. The horn from a logging truck suddenly blared, and then it was like he disappeared.

Kellen and Sasha turned to see a man running towards them. "What the heck is wrong with him?" the newcomer asked. "First, he goes flying by me like all heck's breaking loose, then I hear him crash. Last thing I see is you begging him not to step in front of a truck. I guess he was going to find a way to end it all one way or another."

The highway patrolman took Kellen's statement. He explained that he and Sasha were doing a combination bike/run when he heard the crash and went to investigate. The other witness and the driver of the logging truck corroborated Kellen's story, and it appeared they were free to go.

As Kellen turned to go back to get his bike, he saw Sergeant Murphy pulling over to the crash scene. Glancing at Sasha, he nodded in agreement. "Trouble has arrived."

The Center

Professor Anderson's assistant knocked lightly and entered his office. There's a Sergeant Murphy here to see you. Before he could respond, Murphy stepped in and moved in front of the assistant. She looked at the Professor and said, "There's been an accident."

The assistant gasped and said, "Kellen was out with Sasha. Are they hurt?"

"They are fine, but Officer Janes isn't," Murphy stated. "For reasons that are unclear to me, all of them were at the Brook Nature Reservation. Officer Janes has been hit by a truck and pronounced dead at the scene. He was off duty, but it appears he may have been following Dr. Jackson. We currently have Dr. Jackson down at the station for questioning. We would like you to join us."

Looking at her with his grey eyes, the professor stated, "If we speak to you, it will be here. I also insist Professor Verma and Director Johnston from the DRIA join us."

The Police Station

Kellen and Sasha sat in the conference room where Murphy dropped them after taking his statement about what had happened in the Reservation. It was clear the police were not satisfied with his explanation that Janes was following them and his death was an unfortunate accident. When Kellen suggested he would like a lawyer, or, at the very least, the professors from the Center present, she had sighed and left the room.

Time slowly passed while they waited. Discreetly using sign language to communicate with Sasha, he asked how many people watched through the two-way mirror. She said three and gave the sign to be careful.

When Kellen attempted to leave the room, he found the door locked. He called out, "unless I'm being charged with a crime, I demand to go free." His experience as a man of color was telling him to be patient, but he was having difficulty holding his anger in check. He also wondered who else was watching. There was a camera in the room, and even he could hear people on the other side of the mirror.

Finally, after almost two hours, Murphy returned and said, "You'll accompany me back to the Center."

A voice came over a speaker in the room, "The dog stays here."

"Like hell she does," Kellen stared at the glass as he said it. He then whispered something into Murphy's ear. She nodded and said, "The dog comes with us."

The Center

Murphy, Sasha, and Kellen walked into the main conference room. Already seated at the table were DRIA Director Johnston, Chief of Police Stephen Coates, and Professors Verma and Anderson. Murphy, assuming the meeting was hers, started the discussion.

"Chief Coates, thank you for coming at my request. Director Johnston, you are here at the insistence of Professor Anderson. I appreciate you both taking the time. Today one of my Officers died while evidently conducting surveillance on Dr. Jackson and the dog, Sasha. I know Janes could be overzealous, but I think he knew something. I want to know why he suspected this organization. I want to know why he died. What's going on here?!"

Professor Anderson interrupted, "Please allow me to shed some light on the situation. We are also just putting the pieces together." He clicked a remote, and a picture of Officer Janes came up on the screen.

"Our understanding is Mr. Janes was on temporary assignment filling in for an officer injured while on duty, correct?"

The Chief nodded. "He applied for the position and was imminently qualified. He also had excellent references, which we checked."

An image of Janes' arm then showed on the screen. "This is a tattoo Janes typically kept covered. Our security camera captured this image the night he came to our house when Avi was captured."

Jens continued, "This tattoo is common among members of a group who refer to themselves as 'Separatist Northwest.' Until recently, their primary goal has been to establish a separate sovereign state. This is one of their rallies in Eugene, Oregon." The screen shifted to a group of individuals seemingly chanting. With another click, it zoomed in on one individual.

"That's him! Wow." Murphy said as she shook her head. "How were we not aware of this?"

Director Johnston said, "We think we know. It's true that you checked his references, and his background seemed impeccable. It turns out the numbers you called and the people who answered were fake." Nodding at Professor Anderson, the zoom shifted to another individual. "This same organization also fooled us at the DRIA. This is Agent Williams at the same rally. Surprisingly, he managed to obtain a mid-level security clearance in our organization."

"The rally centered around species purity. The group has shifted its focus to stopping genetic alteration. We think this was how the Faction enlisted their help. With the claimed purpose of eliminating research like that done here, the Faction promoted their true intent of stealing it. They helped place members of the Separatist group inside the local police force and the DRIA. It appears Janes became obsessed with proving Sasha was genetically altered."

Professor Verma spoke for the first time. "Why would he think that? We've been very transparent with all of our reports to the DRIA and," nodding at the Chief, "have an agreement with your department stating we won't allow genetically modified subjects outside the laboratory."

Murphy raised her hand to interrupt. When the Chief nodded, she said, "Janes wasn't the type to believe anything but his own eyes. Also, from the start, he clearly hated Dr. Jackson, the dog, and everything associated with the Center."

Director Johnston nodded at Professor Anderson and continued as the screen shifted to show a satellite view of an encampment. "Based on the information we received from Professor Anderson, we attempted to take Williams into custody, but he has eluded us. We've also started surveillance of Separatists Northwest. Our hope is they can lead us back to the Faction."

Kellen shared a glance with Sasha, both dreading having to share the news of the video with the Professors.

An Undisclosed Location

The trainer was working with Ajax when he saw a text arrive from External Monitoring.

EM: Emailing you a video from the PD resource. Please watch ASAP!

Frustrated by being distracted from his work, the trainer went to his computer and opened the e-mail. As he watched the video, his jaw dropped, and he said, "Holy Crap."

Ajax trotted after his trainer as the man ran toward the front office. Since moving into the new facility, Ajax had tried to see the man referred to as Seven. The trainer knocked respectfully and then closed the door behind him, allowing only a glimpse of the back of his head. Ajax breathed in deep through his nose, noting the elusive man's scent. Listening carefully, he could hear the conversation through the door.

"Mr. Seven, please pardon the intrusion. We just received a video from our resource in the Police Department. You really should see it."

Seven's voice was lower, but Ajax could still make out what he was saying. "Are you sure they are communicating?"

The trainer was excited. "Absolutely. Look, he's talking, and she's responding. Watch this. The dog's communication is beyond Ajax's capabilities."

Ajax felt a moment of indignation before he realized this meant he must be even more careful.

Seven asked the obvious question, "Is there any way a dog without genetic modification could communicate at this level?"

The trainer hesitated, "In my opinion, no."

Seven said, "We need to report this." Ajax heard some noises that sounded like typing on a computer.

A woman's voice said, "Priority code?"

Seven responded with "Alpha One Gold."

She said, "Connecting."

A man's voice said, "What is it?" Seven explained what they had seen in the video. The man asked, "Is the Trainer with you?"

Seven responded, "Under the circumstances, I felt it was necessary. Please elaborate for the Chairman."

The trainer started speaking, his voice betraying how nervous he was. "It was clear the man was speaking to the dog, and it was reacting and responding. This level of communication is beyond the capabilities of Ajax."

As the Chairman responded, Ajax carefully tried to imprint the man's voice in his mind. While not as precise as scent or sight, he believed he could identify him again if he heard him.

"So, you're sure the dog is modified?"

The trainer managed a weak yes and was relieved when Seven said, "Thank you for bringing this to our attention. Please leave now."

Ajax moved away from the door as the trainer returned to the reception area. Thankfully, the trainer decided to take a moment to collect himself by sinking into one of the chairs and jotting some notes into a pad he carried. Ajax tried to look nonchalant as he turned his right ear to focus on listening to what was happening in the office. His acute hearing was just able to pick up an alarming exchange.

Seven's voice, ".....data captured appears to have been fabricated."

Chairman's voice, "<garbled> implement extraction protocol. We want all of the researchers and the dog."

Seven's voice, "And the two children?"

The trainer got up to leave, making it difficult for Ajax to hear the Chairman's response. The one word he did hear was "leverage." Ajax knew it was time to leave.

Home

After the police had left, Director Johnston had asked to speak with Professors Anderson and Verma alone. Kellen and Sasha walked Avi and Noah home. When they finally reached the Anderson house, he recounted the entire day from the morning's events through the meeting that had just ended. Both Noah and Avi gasped when they heard Janes had recorded Sasha communicating with Kellen.

"But you didn't tell the police or DRIA?" Noah asked as he unconsciously put his hand on Sasha's shoulder.

Kellen grimaced, "I know. I lied to the DRIA and the police. But if I hadn't, Sasha would have been exposed."

Noah shrugged, "I guess we've deceived them about Sasha from the beginning. I'm starting to realize some goals supersede the rules and regulations of the bureaucracies around us. I understand people's fear of genetically modified species, but in this case, there's no fear of the genetics getting out of control. To be honest, I was always a bit worried about the smart mice escaping, but not you!" He smiled at Sasha, who made a growly face to show she could be scary. Everyone laughed.

Avi smiled, "After meeting Ajax, I have no worries about that either. But I do wonder what would happen if you and Ajax....you know."

Sasha feigned ignorance, but she had felt something upon seeing Ajax. It was the first time they had been together since she was a puppy. She pushed the thoughts out of her mind. There was no way of knowing if they would ever see each other again.

Noah, seeing her discomfort, changed the subject to the more pressing matter. "So, do you think the video made it to the Faction?"

At that moment, the two professors walked through the door. Carefully closing it, Noah's father said, "What video?" As Kellen explained, the Professors exchanged a glance. Noah's father said, "Let's move to the three-season room to talk."

Once they were all comfortably seated in the room overlooking the backyard, Noah's dad told the group what they had heard from Director Johnston. "As you all heard, the DRIA has been monitoring the activities of the Separatist Northwest. Their analysts report increased activity in the group's camp after the Janes incident. This activity continued for 90 minutes when the entire camp appears to have dismantled itself. The camp and everyone in it have disappeared."

Kellen shook his head, thinking of Janes, "These don't seem to be the type of people to give up. What does the DRIA think is going on?"

Avi's mom provided the answer. "The DRIA believes that either the Separatist's leadership or The Faction realized that we knew about

Janes and Williams. The consensus among the Analysts is both groups are going underground. Jens and I have drawn our own conclusions but want to know what the rest of you think."

Noah took the lead, "The Faction is coming for us. They know we lied, and I would guess their patience is gone. They don't want the Separatists around to learn more about their true agenda, so they convinced them to go underground."

Avi nodded, "The Faction isn't going to slow down. They want to accelerate their efforts."

"What about Ajax?" Kellen directed the question to Avi. "Will he help them? What's his unfinished business?"

Before Avi could answer, Sasha reacted. Kellen said, "Are you sure your emotions aren't clouding your judgment?" Sasha's reaction caused him to backpedal, "Okay! I get it." She gave him a quick head butt to apologize for her "outburst."

Noah looked to his father, "So we know they're coming. Is it time?"

Jens looked to Indira and Kellen, who both nodded. He then said, "Prepare to evacuate, but use Option 3."

In the last few months, the group had discussed the possible need to flee the lab. They had developed multiple options. Option 3 had the group breaking into two parties of 3. Noah, his father, and Sasha were in one group, while Avika, her mother, and Kellen were in the second group. Each of the potential pairs in the group also had a contingency plan. The key was the plans were only known to the group members who had made them. The idea was a last-ditch effort to prevent the Faction from capturing one team member and then using him/her to find the others. Plans had been put in place, making it possible for the groups to rejoin once it was deemed safe.

Noah said, "But we're not leaving right away, right?"

Avi's mom answered, "We need a little more time to prepare. I'm hoping we have at least a few more days, but if we have to, we could leave immediately." Then looking to Avi, she said, "It's been quite a day. Let's all head home."

An Undisclosed Location

The trainer escorted Ajax to his room. The German Shepherd inwardly groaned, seeing the bowls of kibble and water on the floor. The trainer ruffled his ears as Ajax carefully looked at the piece of cardboard strategically placed by the door. As the trainer left, the door started to close. At the last second, Ajax grabbed the cardboard in his teeth and slid it between the door and frame. The mechanism had pulled the door shut, but the cardboard was just strong enough to prevent the latch from engaging.

Ajax had confirmed that the doors could all be monitored from the central security station, unlike at the previous training facility. Fortunately, it seemed the guards didn't bother to check the internal doors showing unlocked alarms on their monitors. He had practiced this several times in the past, and no one seemed to notice. He expected tonight would be no different. In two hours, everyone would be gone except the night guards. He settled in and started to chew the elk antler his trainer had left him, a nervous "dog habit" that helped him calm his nerves and focus on his plan.

As Seven left the building, he checked in with Security one last time. The guard said, "All good," and looked back down at his magazine. Seven pointed at the screen and said, "What about that alarm?"

The guard looked and said, "It's just an interior door. Protocol is it's supposed to be locked, but it sometimes gives a false alarm. It happens every so often."

Seven shook his head. "This doesn't feel right. I want to check it with you."

The guard radioed one of the two roving security men. When the man arrived to cover the front desk, Seven followed the guard to the door. As they proceeded through the facility, everything seemed to be as expected. The door that was showing unlocked appeared closed, but he asked the guard to open it. The guard put his key in the lock and left the entire ring there. Stepping into the room, he said, "See nothing here."

Ajax heard them coming down the hall long before they arrived. By the sound of the steps, he could tell it was two men. When they spoke outside his door, he realized one of them was the one they called Seven. He moved behind the door, so he wouldn't be visible as it opened. The guard entered the room and said, "See nothing here." Seven followed him through the doorway, just into the room. Ajax let out a growl that sounded like a roar. Leaping at the guard, he knocked him down. As Ajax turned toward Seven, he saw the guard's radio on the floor and pushed it toward the door with his rear paw.

Seven was astonished as he saw the enormous black animal attack the guard. He instinctively fought to get back through the door. As he heard the guard's radio clatter by his feet, he felt the animal hit his legs. Falling to one knee, he now realized it was Ajax. He ducked as Ajax jumped over him and out the door. Seven grabbed the edge of the door and quickly swung it shut. As he heard the door slam, he realized they were safe from Ajax but were now locked in the room.

Ajax stopped and looked at the door. The keys had been knocked out of the lock and were lying on the floor. He carefully picked these up with his teeth and dropped them in a trash bin filled with papers. By shaking it a bit, he was able to make the keys slide out of sight. Ajax picked the radio up and, moving carefully to avoid being seen by a camera, carried it to a bucket of dirty water the janitors had been using to clean the floor. As he dropped it in, he wondered if the shift still consisted of the four security officers, as he had read earlier on the schedule.

The man temporarily staffing the front desk attempted to call his colleague who had gone to check the door. When he didn't answer, he tried to locate him on the cameras but couldn't find him anywhere. He called the other roving guard and asked him to check it out. "He's probably just in the bathroom, but we should make sure he hasn't slipped and fallen or something."

Ajax knew that a man was assigned to watch the front and rear entrances at all times. Since one guard was locked in with Seven, there should be only one more guard to address before reaching the reception area. He didn't have long to wait as the man came around the corner. Ajax hid and allowed the guard to approach the door containing the men trapped inside.

The roving guard could detect muffled voices coming from one of the doors. When he answered these, he was surprised to hear the voice of the man called Seven say, "Get us out of here!"

"Sorry, Sir, the only set of keys is at the front desk. I'll be right back!"

Seven tried to get the guard to stop by yelling, "Wait!" but sensed he was already gone. He knew the keys had to be right by the door, but the guard hadn't seen them.

Ajax watched as the guard hurried toward the front desk. The shortest way there was to cut through the training area. The previous day Ajax had been practicing a sequence of escapes from a deep pit in the building's center. The various objects he used had been removed, but the hole was still uncovered.

As the guard skirted near the edge, Ajax appeared suddenly out of the shadows, growling loudly. Terrified, the man attempted to call for help on his radio. Ajax charged him, knocking the radio out of his hands and sending the man back against the rope protecting the pit. The man's attempt to grab the rope was futile, and he fell back screaming. A thick pad in the bottom had saved the man's life, but as he lay groaning, it was clear he wasn't going anywhere soon.

At the front desk and rear entrance, the two remaining men had heard a quick desperate call for help on their radios. When they could not raise any of the other guards, the front desk guard called for outside backup. As soon as the security company dispatcher answered, the front desk guard exclaimed, "the facility is under attack! Send a team immediately!"

Hanging up the phone, he knew protocol was to initiate a lockdown. He was just about to do that when the huge black dog appeared from the lab area. The beast was staring at him and growling low and deep. He and the other guards had always been terrified of the animal. Deciding living was more important than locking down the lab, he jumped over the desk in an attempt to reach the bathroom. He yelled, "Oh shit!" as the dog leaped over a table and came at him.

As Ajax entered the reception area, his concern was the remaining guard would lock down the facility. He decided his best bet was to get the man away from the desk. Charging toward the man, Ajax knew it would be simple to catch the lumbering guard, but the easier option was to allow him to get away and hide.

The guard ran into the bathroom, and Ajax heard the door lock. He also heard him call for help on his radio. Turning to the exit, he was thankful the doors had automatic openers, and neither of the remaining guards had managed to execute a lockdown. Stepping outside, he felt the cool night air on his fur. As he heard the security patrol cars approaching, he disappeared into the wooded lot. For the first time in years, he was free.

The Chairman's Office

The Chairman looked up as his assistant entered after a light knock.

"Excuse me, Sir. We have a call. Alpha One Gold."

The Chairman attempted to hide his surprise. Yesterday's call was only the second of this code he had ever received. To get another this soon seemed inconceivable. His role as head of the National Technology Security Council provided him access to all of the latest R&D efforts funded by the federal government. Consequently, he often had communications with the highest security clearance. But most of his Faction-related communication he attempted to complete using other means.

"Please set up the secure line, and ensure no one interrupts." The Chairman was already turning away from the assistant as he gave the command.

Once the connection was complete, he announced his presence in his usual fashion.

"Report"

On the other side of the line, Seven hesitated before saying, "We have a situation. Ajax has escaped from our facility."

"WHAT?!" This was a catastrophe. The Faction had made him the Chairman based on his access to cutting-edge technology development and his ability to harness this in their R&D projects. While there were setbacks on occasion, this was the first of this nature. He cringed at the thought of reporting this event at the next meeting with the Board he chaired.

"How did it happen?"

"I was present when he escaped." Seven realized he might be signing his death warrant. "It appears Ajax engineered the escape himself."

"How? He's a dog!" The Chairman corrected himself. "I realize he is brilliant and capable, but how is this possible?"

Seven's voice betrayed his excitement, "That's the interesting part. It appears his intelligence and capabilities are greater than we realized. I've reviewed the actions he took, and it's quite astounding."

He explained all of Ajax's actions, including the part where Ajax trapped him and the guard. His hope was the excitement of the possibility overrode the Chairman's anger over the loss. Hearing only silence from the Chairman, he paused.

Weighing his words carefully, the Chairman finally said, "This has immense implications. The Board are individuals of vision and have invested in us heavily. They'll be extremely interested, but we must have the basis for the technology. Capture the scientists who made this possible. Do it now!"

"What about the dogs?" Seven then added, "and the children?"

The Chairman took only a moment, "As we discussed earlier, the children provide leverage to keep their parents cooperative. The dogs are excellent examples of the technology, but based on what you just told me, they appear to be uncontrollable. We should be able to create our own animals who will be loyal to us."

Seven said merely, "Understood."

The Academy

Several days had passed with no response from the Faction. Noah and Avi were in their leadership class when Principal Banks entered, looking flustered. As she and Professor Feinberg spoke, she glanced at them. Exchanging a look, Noah and Avi got a sinking feeling when the principal turned and gestured to them.

"Avi, Noah, I need you to come to the office with me." After they joined her at the front of the room, she said quietly, "Evidently there's been an incident involving your parents at the Center. Some men from the Department of Defense are here to take you over to them."

Avi asked, "Are they okay? Did they tell you anything more?"

Ms. Banks shook her head. "They didn't indicate that anyone's hurt. They did say there are security clearance issues, and the situation is sensitive."

As they walked to the principal's office, Noah could see the agents standing in the outer reception area. As one of them turned, Noah recognized Agent Williams. He signaled

Avi to look, and he could see she recognized him too.

"Principal Banks, before we go to the Center, I need to grab some things from my gym locker."

"Noah, whatever it is, it can wait. These men are insistent."

"It's my access card to the Lab. We may need it. I'll be right back."

Before she could object further, Noah was gone. He ran into the locker room, and as he had hoped, Alex and Joe were there getting ready for gym class.

"Guys, listen. I can't talk long, and you have to trust me. Some men are here, and they are pretending to be from the DOD. They are trying to kidnap Avi and me."

Unlike most people, Alex didn't object or ask for details. He simply asked, "How can we help?"

Noah outlined the plan and hoped they could provide the distraction he and Avi needed. Then he grabbed the access badge from his locker and rejoined Avi and the principal.

As the three of them walked into the reception area, the man they knew as Agent Williams turned to greet them.

"Noah, Avi. I'm sorry to alarm you. As I'm sure you recall, I'm Agent Williams. A routine security check revealed both of you might have been exposed to some confidential information. We want to take you over to the

Lab so we can discuss this with your parents. We just want to ensure it doesn't happen again in the future."

Avi looked at Noah, who was signaling her to "go along." When she said, "Sure, we're always looking for a reason to get out of class," Williams visibly relaxed.

"Great, it's a nice day, so we figured we could just walk over to the Center." Williams continued to chat with them, wanting to appear accommodating. As the fake agent held the door, Noah caught him exchanging a look with the other two men before saying to the principal, "This may take a bit, so I wouldn't expect Noah and Avi to be back today."

Principal Banks stepped in front of the group. "Wait! You didn't mention that you were taking them out of the school. I'll need to come with you."

Williams pretended to be agreeable. "That's fine until we get over to the Center with their parents." He signaled the other men to follow as they left the building. Walking on the sidewalk toward the campus, the "agent" continued to chat with the principal, but Noah caught him looking toward the visitor parking lot where one of the other men had gone to move their van to the Center.

The sidewalk turned, and they started walking alongside the recreational fields where Joe was engaged in pitching practice with Alex. Noah signaled "get ready" to Avi. Joe appeared to pause to let them pass by, but as they walked behind Alex, he suddenly wound up. Noah was amazed at how the fastball made Agent Williams' head snap back. As Williams dropped to the ground like a rock, the other man started to reach into his jacket.

Knowing what was about to happen with the pitch, Alex picked up the bat and was already pivoting toward the group when he saw the man reaching for something. He brought the bat around in a near-perfect swing, striking the man on the elbow. The connection made a solid "THOCK," and the gun clattered to the ground as the man shouted in pain.

Noah heard the van's engine racing as the third man drove across the lawn toward them. He saw Joe had already made it to the locker room door about 30 yards away. Alex had grabbed the hand of the shocked principal and was guiding her to the same destination. Once through the door, they were to close it, and it would automatically lock.

Knowing their friends were safe, Avi and Noah sprinted toward the entrance to the cross country trail. It led to a network of paths in the University woods they knew from their training runs with Kellen. They heard the van pause as the man stopped to pick up his injured comrades before driving directly across the grass towards them. Already panting, the two children had just reached the entrance when the van skidded to a halt just behind them.

The driver jumped out of the van, and Williams groggily followed. The two of them started running in pursuit. Glancing back, Noah noticed the third man who got hit by Alex appeared to fall out of the van and was on his hands and knees vomiting. Coming to a fork, Noah signaled Avi that they should split up.

Both Noah and Avi were about fifteen yards ahead of the fresher pursuers, who were not as fit or dressed to run in the woods. Noah planned to stay far enough away to prevent getting grabbed, but close enough to keep them engaged and to wear them down. He and Avi would then rejoin and sprint to the Center.

Noah felt like he was flowing like water over the rocks and obstacles as he ran through the trails. The endurance training with Kellen was paying off. The driver was chasing him and was having a hard time keeping up. As the man stumbled and cursed behind him, Noah decided to try something different.

Veering off the main path, Noah ran down a small side trail. Allowing the man to get a bit closer, Noah had to jump from rock to rock to cross a small stream and duck to avoid branches. He almost allowed the man to get too close at one point when the man lurched forward and just missed grabbing his shirt. The man yelled, "I'm going to get you, you #$%$#."

The trail took a sudden turn to the left and quickly dropped five feet. It traversed a small ravine by way of a rotted, makeshift bridge.

Noah knew it was possible to cross by stepping precisely on the spot in the middle where the planks were supported from below. At his current speed and with the trail's slight decline, Noah's foot hit harder than usual. His breath caught as he heard the wood crack. Somehow it held, and his next step took him across. A second later, the man came down the hill.

The man's foot hit the bridge just short of the support. The wood seemed to disintegrate below him. Pitching forward as he fell through the opening, the man tried to get his hands in front of him. Noah was shocked to see his face hit the broken edge of the bridge. Knocked unconscious, or perhaps worse, the man slid down into the ravine, motionless. Noah paused only for a moment before his thoughts returned to Avi. He sprinted back to the main trail.

Noah raced to get to the crossover point where he had hoped to meet Avi. Just before his trail joined hers, he was distressed to see her just ahead of Agent Williams. What was worse, Williams still appeared to be running well.

Noah attempted to get Agent Williams to follow him instead. Calling out, "OVER HERE!" he was dismayed to see Avi look at him as well. A root caught her toe, and she fell forward. Williams exclaimed, "Yes!" as he closed in to grab the girl.

Williams' jubilation was short-lived as the brush next to him seemed to explode. The growl sounded terrifying as Ajax plowed into the unsuspecting man. Tumbling over, Williams was able to get his gun out and was just bringing it to bear when Ajax hit him again. The shot rang out, and Ajax yelped as it hit him. His momentum knocked Williams down, sending the gun flying. Before Williams could react again, Ajax's jaws were on his neck. As the man tried to grab something to fight him off, Officer Murphy stepped onto the path with her gun leveled. She yelled out a command, "WAIT!"

As Murphy secured Williams' hands with handcuffs, Noah and Avi looked in awe at Ajax walking toward them. Avi let out a small noise and wrapped her arms around his neck. Sobbing, she buried her head in his fur. Finally pulling back, she said, "Sorry, it's just that when I saw him shoot, I thought I had lost you!"

Murphy said, "It looks like he got lucky. Just a minor wound on his left shoulder. Good thing your principal made that 911 call." Looking at Williams, she added, "I think we have a lot to talk about. Your friend back at the van is in a lot of pain and has already started to sing."

Williams smirked, "I doubt it. And this is far from over."

Noah said, "If you mean the guy who was chasing me, he's back in the ravine in pretty bad shape." As Williams continued to smile, Noah turned back to Murphy, "Did you send anyone to the Center?"

"Why would we do that?" as Murphy asked the question, she noticed Williams' smile involuntarily widen. She grabbed her radio as Noah, Avi, and Ajax were already sprinting down the path.

The Center

The van pulled up directly in front of the Center. Three men dressed in black tactical clothes and dark sunglasses were out and walking through the front door within seconds. The security guard at the front desk stood up and could not even speak before the Taser electrodes hit him. The leader pushed his limp body aside, deactivated the camera system, and unlocked all doors in the facility.

One of the men went through the door that entered the back of the lab. The leader and the third man moved through the hallway to the offices. Turning to the right, the leader stopped just outside Professor Verma's door. He took a quick look using a small mirror, then pulled back and signaled the number one with his index finger. The other man pulled out what looked like a pistol and positioned himself by the door.

He turned and walked back towards Professor Anderson's door. Checking with the mirror, he confirmed the man was also seated at his desk. From his position, he could see both office doors and the entrance to the lab. He readied himself by Anderson's door and waited.

The man who had entered the lab silently emerged from it. He signaled zero, confirming their intel was correct that the dog and the researcher named Kellen weren't there. The leader nodded and looked back towards the man by Professor Verma's door. Holding up three fingers, he evenly counted down: three, two, one.

On the count of one, both men pivoted into the door frames. As the two professors looked up, they were simultaneously hit in the neck by tranquilizer darts.

The man who had been in the lab pushed a large cart down the hall. He and the leader loaded the two unconscious professors and then carried them to the back loading dock. The van was already there waiting for them. Within seconds the men loaded the professors on stretchers in the back, their arms and legs restrained.

As the driver pulled away from the dock, the leader pulled out his phone and dialed a number. "Alpha team reports success." He hung up and pulled the SIM card out of the phone. After breaking it, he wiped it and the phone off and tossed both into some bushes on the side of the road.

The Brook Nature Reservation

Kellen smiled as he and his bike glided through a flowy section of trail in the reservation. It was a perfect morning with the temperature just slightly crisp. Sasha was running up ahead of him, and they were both reveling in their little bit of freedom from the lab and her training.

Everything changed as he powered up a small hill. At the top, he noticed a sudden change in her attitude as she signaled danger and jumped to the side of the trail into the bushes. The crack of a rifle shot sounded. Kellen dove off his bike, following Sasha into the scrub.

The shooter had been waiting for nearly 20 minutes. The Alpha team leader had briefed him that his targets typically would take a break from the lab mid-morning. The two of them would either go for a run or ride nearby. The entire operation was initiated when the targets were seen leaving the lab. As the two other teams started their missions to get the children and Professors, he alone had followed the dog and scientist.

Riding his bike slightly behind them, he was relieved when they headed to the Reservation. As they started their outing, he cut over to a hill near the end of the trail. He had scouted this position carefully and knew it provided the best opportunity to take out the dog as it came up the rise. After assembling the rifle from the pack on his back, he patiently waited until he heard them coming. As the dog came up over the rise below, he took a breath and started to let it out when the dog suddenly jumped to the side. He took the shot but immediately realized it was a miss. Gritting his teeth, he hid the rifle in some underbrush and pulled out his pistol. He silently moved down the hill.

Kellen crawled in the bushes over to Sasha. He whispered, "Are you okay?" and saw her response requesting silence. He watched her ears rotate as she tried to detect the assailant. She pointed in a direction, but Kellen couldn't see or hear anything. Following her, they moved forward, so they were beyond the point where she expected the man to emerge.

The man eased back down the hill to the path, listening to hear Kellen and the dog. He was pretty sure they hadn't moved far and were trying to figure out his location. He planned to get across the path and step out on a large boulder that was tall enough to give him a view of the brushy area where they were hiding. Since they were unarmed, he wasn't concerned about them seeing him. He would then shoot the dog and tranquilize the man.

Kellen and Sasha made it beyond the rock and were actually behind the man as he stepped onto the boulder. They were banking on the man's expectation they wouldn't travel towards danger. Sasha was trying to get back on the main path and slip away while the assailant searched for them in the underbrush. Only steps from the man, it appeared this would work when Kellen's foot slid, making a soft crunching noise.

The man pivoted and aimed the gun at Sasha. Kellen reacted protectively by stepping in front of her. Sasha watched as the gun went off and Kellen fell. A crimson spot appeared on Kellen's chest. Fueled by rage, she charged the man as he attempted to get the gun aimed at her. His hesitation saved her life and cost him his, as her impact knocked the gun up towards his face. She heard the gun fire again and felt the man fall below her. He wouldn't be getting up.

Sasha looked back at Kellen and used her rear paw to activate the emergency beacon Kellen had installed in her collar. The signal would go to Noah, his father, and Kellen's phone. She heard the alarm sound on Kellen's phone, confirming the system was working. Crawling over, she put her body against his and hoped help would arrive soon.

The Academy

Noah, Avi, and Detective Murphy had just emerged from the trail when Noah's phone signaled an alarm.

"Oh NO! It's Sasha!" Noah brought up his GPS tracking app. Sasha and Kellen were together in the Brook Reservation. Showing

Avi and Murphy the location, he asked, "She'd only use this if they were in trouble. What can we do?"

"Get me the chopper!" Murphy was already on the phone with dispatch. She provided the GPS coordinates and said, "Details are unclear, but expect possible armed suspects and injuries." Murphy pointed to her SUV, "Let's go!"

Noah and Avi climbed in the rear seat while Murphy opened the rear hatch for Ajax. Within seconds they were on their way, lights flashing and sirens blaring. Once they were on the road, Noah and Avi tried to call his father and her mother. Both phones went straight to voicemail. Calling out to Murphy over the noise, Avi yelled, "WE CAN'T REACH MY MOM OR NOAH'S DAD! HAS ANYONE CHECKED THE CENTER YET?"

Murphy switched off the siren and slowed slightly. She quickly called dispatch and asked for the status from the officers dispatched to check on the professors. Noah and Avi could hear the response indicating no one was at the Center when officers arrived. A patrol car was checking their houses. Noah looked at Avi and shook his head. She signaled him back with three fingers. They needed to get Sasha and Kellen and flee.

Dispatch came back on the radio. "Helicopter has arrived on the scene. Code 123."

Noah asked Murphy, "What's that mean?"

"It means there's an injury." Murphy stared ahead. "Brace yourselves."

The Brook Nature Reservation

When the SUV pulled into the reservation parking lot, they saw the State Police helicopter and an ambulance already there. As Murphy opened the door, an officer walked over to apprise her of the situation. Although the police officers tried to speak softly, Avi and Noah heard, "one deceased, one chest wound." They noticed Ajax running toward the ambulance.

Sasha was standing by the ambulance, watching over Kellen in the back as they made the final preparations to take him to the hospital. She heard the SUV pull in and was relieved to see Noah and Avi climb out. As Murphy spoke to the officer in charge, the rear gate of the vehicle opened, and, to her surprise, Ajax jumped out. For just a moment, she forgot about Kellen and her fear he may not make it. Ajax looked incredible as he trotted toward her. She felt emotions she never knew existed but quickly put them aside as she heard the ambulance pulling away.

Using their unique language, Sasha communicated to Ajax that Kellen was seriously injured and on the way to the hospital. Smelling and seeing the blood on him, she asked what happened. Before he could answer, one of the EMTs, who had stayed behind, walked over.

"Hey there, looks like you're bleeding. Murphy radioed that a dog had been shot, so I stayed behind. Don't worry. I'm in Vet school as well as an EMT." Pulling out some scissors, he quickly trimmed the fur where the bullet had struck Ajax.

"Wow, you won the lottery on this one. It appears to have just grazed your shoulder. I'm going to shave this little spot, clean it, and give you a quick stitch or two. I'm sure it stings." Ajax held stock still and didn't even wince as the EMT finished administering the first aid.

Looking at Avi, the EMT said, "Wow, he's a trooper. I wish I could have him in my practicum demonstrations. Put some of this antibiotic on twice a day for the next ten days. The stitches can come out then."

When the EMT left, Noah and Avi discretely communicated with Ajax and Sasha. As Sasha updated, Noah quietly relayed what had happened to Kellen. When she described the wound, Noah was unable to contain his dismay. Turning to Avi, he said, "It's worse than the officers said. Sasha says Kellen is in bad shape. Her read of the EMTs reactions is they think he won't make it."

"Does anyone know where my mom and your dad are?" Avi's voice was shaking. Ajax stepped next to her. He leaned slightly against her, and she appreciated the support. She held the three signal, and Noah nodded.

Murphy and the others were busy with multiple crime scenes and suspects in custody. The man who had chased Noah was also pronounced dead on the scene, so her resources were heavily divided. Almost an hour went by before she thought to check in with Noah and Avi. When she couldn't find them by the SUV, she checked with the other officers. No one knew where they were. They had vanished.

An Undisclosed Location

Seven knew he had to provide an update to the Chairman, but he wasn't sure what his reaction would be. The two primary researchers were currently locked inside their cells, and most of the unedited lab notebooks and reports had been recovered. The third researcher was in a coma and unlikely to recover, which was unfortunate, but they did have his work.

The issue was the children and the dogs had not been captured yet. He decided he would present the overall outcome as a success and that the search for the children was underway. He clicked the link, and the chatbox opened.

Chairman: Report.

Seven: Alpha team has successfully extracted the two primary researchers. The third scientist was severely injured.

Chairman: Is he essential to our endeavor?

Seven: No. His primary contribution was to train the dogs and their handlers. We have his notes and believe our techniques are superior.

Chairman: The children and the dogs?

Seven: They managed to elude us. We are in pursuit and should be able to capture them soon.

Chairman: Let's hope so. Keep me apprised.

PART 4

Alex's House

When they split up, Noah and Sasha slipped away on one of the trails that cut through the Reservation. Noah knew it linked to a small subdivision where Alex lived. It was clear they couldn't return to the campus or their house any time soon. They hoped no one would notice they were missing for a while, but their time was limited. Hopefully, Alex was home and could get them started on their escape.

As they reached Alex's house, luck was with them since he was in his driveway practicing free throws. His greeting of "Hey guys!" was quickly silenced by Noah, and he gathered something was up. They stepped inside his family's garage and closed the door.

"Alex, listen closely. We have to hurry. Kellen's been shot. My dad and Avi's mom are missing. I need help getting away."

After taking a moment to digest what he had just heard, Alex replied, "The police are watching me like hawks. I just got back from the station. They seem to drive by every five minutes. They think breaking one of the bad guy's arms puts me at risk. If I ask my mom to give you a ride, she'll want to call your dad and then the police."

Noah nodded and noticed Alex's bikes hanging in the back of the garage. "How close does the bike path come to your house?" Then turning to Sasha, he asked, "Can you run ten miles? I know you've already run quite a bit today."

Alex smiled, "The bike path runs right behind us. We don't even have to go out on the road if we cut through the Simmons' yard. They're not home. As for you," he paused to put his hand on Sasha, "My dad bought a trailer so we can ride with our dog, Buck. I think you'll fit fine."

Alex pulled down two bicycles. One was his current gravel bike. The other was a smaller road bike he had outgrown. As he hooked the trailer up, Sasha looked at it warily.

Noticing her apprehension, Alex said, "Don't worry, it's comfortable and safe." Smiling at Noah, he added, "And this will slow me down enough so you might be able to keep up."

Noah rolled his eyes as Sasha continued to stare at the contraption suspiciously.

She balked when Alex tried to put a pair of sunglasses and a helmet on her. Noah signaled, "Please?" When she gave in, she realized they were made for a dog her size and were actually quite comfortable.

Rolling down the bike path with her head sticking out, sunglasses and helmet on, she realized she was quite a sight. But, she did have to admit the gear was a good disguise. Once she got comfortable, the ride was pretty enjoyable.

The bike path ended at the local commuter rail station. Alex quickly broke the extra bike down and managed to get it in the trailer. Giving Noah all the money he had, he hugged him and said, "I know you can't tell me where you're going, but you know how to reach me. I'll help in any way that I can." He pushed his head against Sasha's one last time before he turned and pedaled toward home.

The Highway

After they watched Noah and Sasha slip away, Ajax looked to Avi for guidance. She said very softly, "We need to reach the highway. I'm going to use the plan Kellen and I had for getting away." Waiting until everyone was distracted, Ajax led her down a path opposite from Sasha and Noah's. After walking about a mile, he suddenly cut off the trail and entered the woods.

The underbrush was dense, but there was a rough trail heading in the direction they were going. Hearing the hum of traffic a couple hundred yards away, Avi signaled for Ajax to stop. Pulling out a disposable phone Kellen had provided, she powered it on. There was one number in the contact list. Per Kellen's instructions, she sent a text providing the location of the pickup. She selected a mile marker she had noticed on the way into the reserve.

A: RT 24. Marker 257.

The response took about two minutes that seemed forever in the buggy, closed underbrush.

P: 15 min. Alternating directional.

Not quite knowing what the text meant, they continued out to the highway. Upon reaching the grassy area beside the road, Avi realized they were a good quarter mile from the marker. Cutting back into the brush, they made their way closer, but Avi realized they weren't going to make it to the rendezvous point before the 15 minutes was up. She decided to sprint the last 100 yards in the open grass when her contact arrived.

She didn't have long to wait as a non-descript silver car pulled over into the breakdown lane with its directional signals alternating between right and left every few seconds. As she sprinted out, the man stopped and reached back to open the rear door. As he pulled back out onto the highway, he said, "Stay down, Statey up ahead."

Avi and Ajax ducked down as they heard the state trooper pull onto the highway, siren blaring. The Officer went back towards town as they proceeded by the Reservation's entrance at just slightly above the speed limit. Once things appeared safe, the man said, "Where's Kellen?"

Avi's voice cracked as she explained that he had been shot. The man nodded, and when she tried to catch his eye in the mirror, he said, "Let's not see each other, okay? Also, Kellen didn't mention the dog."

"Sorry! It was a change of plan." She stammered, "I'm really sorry."

She saw the man's head nod, "Good thing I like dogs...and kids. If Kellen hadn't said 'trust,' I wouldn't do this. I don't want to help some kid run away. But I sense it ain't like that."

As Avi thought of her mom and Kellen, she finally let herself cry. "No, it's not. I'd do anything to be home right now."

After several hours of driving, Avi felt the car stop. Shaking off sleep, she sat up to see they had stopped in front of a small wharf. There wasn't much around, but there was a diner across the street. Her growling stomach reminded her that she hadn't eaten since breakfast. Avi was happy to reach their first stop but wasn't sure what to do next.

"Here, Kid." The driver handed back a wad of bills. "Kellen said if you were alone, I should text a number saying you arrived. That's done. I don't know anything more than that. I suspect your next contact will find you. It's all I've got. I wish I could do more."

She held back a tear, thanked the man, and got out of the vehicle with Ajax. In a moment of panic, she realized she didn't even know what town this was. She looked down at Ajax, who was stoic, and she pointed at the diner. Hardening her resolve, she walked across the street as the car pulled away.

The Diner

A bell rang as the door opened, and a grandmotherly woman called out, "Be right with you." As Avi waited, she noticed the "NO PETS" sign. Looking down at Ajax, she could tell he had read it, too, and his body was in a slightly aggressive stance. The smell of food from the grill made her stomach grumble, and she wondered when Ajax had last had a meal.

When the woman finally came over, she took a look at Ajax and said to Avi, "Honey, we'll have you eat in the outdoor area, if that's okay." Avi nodded and followed her. They went out back to a small area that was outdoors but covered. The woman flipped a sign on the door reading "Section Closed" and brought them to a table where a blanket and bowl of cool water were already laid out for Ajax.

"My name's Ruby. Kellen had contacted me a while back and said you might come through needing help. The only thing you need to know is I'm a friend who'd do anything for that young man. Now, before we get started, I suspect you and your handsome friend are hungry. I don't have much in the way of dog food, but I have the cook making up a big batch of grilled chicken and boiled rice."

As Ajax's mouth watered, he couldn't help but give a big thump with his tail. "I swear he understands every word I say." Ruby smiled at Ajax. "Sorry about the 'No Pets' thing. Me, I personally like dogs more than people." She looked back at Avi, "We have things to discuss, but first some food?"

Avi nodded and asked for a burger and some fries. After she left, Avi made a face at Ajax. "Guess you'll have to just do without kibble tonight." Ajax bumped her with his head. "Yeah, we have to figure out how to improve our communication."

Ruby came back and said, "The order is in and should be up pronto. Meanwhile, this is a box Kellen had left with me. He told me to give it to you if you should pass through."

Avi waited until she left to open the box. On top was an envelope addressed to her. Opening it, she found a note from Kellen.

Avi,

If you're reading this, something has happened to separate us. I've asked the woman who runs this diner to help you. Ruby is a friend from my earlier life who you can trust completely. I've instructed her to get you on the local ferry that goes up the coast. You should get off at the third stop where you'll meet your next contact. I've put some things in the box you might find helpful. Also, there is a general store at the ferry stop with almost anything you might need.

Take care and hope to see you soon,

Kellen

PS. Here is the training book I put together for Sasha's sign language. Just in case you need something to keep you busy. :^)

Avi wiped a tear away and whispered, "Hope to see you soon, too...." She showed the letter to Ajax and looked through the box. She found another disposable phone, the book, a backpack, and a ticket for the ferry with a pamphlet showing the stops. There was a billfold containing several thousand dollars.

Ruby came out with their food. The smell was overwhelming, and both of the travelers couldn't wait to get at it. Seeing their expressions, she said, "You two look like you should focus on eating. I'll be back to talk in a little bit."

The food tasted incredible and was topped off when she came out with a bowl of blueberry cobbler. As Avi ate it, she shared some whipped cream with Ajax. Ruby went to the door and made sure she latched it before coming back to speak in a low voice with Avi. "Other than the box, Kellen asked me to do one other thing for you. He wanted me to help you get on the Ferry."

The Airports

Noah and Sasha took the train several stops and exited just before it went inside the inner beltway. Walking a few blocks, he came to one of the chain fitness gyms. Flashing a membership card, he asked the attractive woman at the desk if his dog could wait with her in the reception area while he retrieved his bag.

Sasha did her equivalent of an eye roll when he said "Stay" and loosely tied a makeshift leash made from his belt to a chair. He ran in and quickly pulled his "go bag" from the locker he had rented months ago. Noah had paid a year's membership in advance under a false identity just to keep it here. He got back out to reception just as some people started to come up to Sasha.

After explaining that yes, she was a German Shepherd, and no, white was really not uncommon, he quickly exited the building. Walking over to a coffee shop with outdoor seating, he replaced his belt-leash with a real one. He also put Sasha in a service dog vest he had bought on the internet. Then, pulling out a laptop, he got on the local Wi-Fi and purchased two first-class tickets to Providenciales, the largest island of the Turks and Caicos archipelago, under his new identity. He specified he was traveling with a service dog.

Navigating the commuter rail and subways, Noah and Sasha made it to the airport in just a little over an hour. Checking in at the gate and getting his documents cleared was, to his surprise, not difficult since his new identification said he was 15. His first real test was going through the security checkpoint. He wondered if the TSA agent would question him traveling out of the country alone at age 15. He waited until he saw a middle-aged couple walking toward the Preferred Traveler line and, giving Sasha the "look cute" sign, walked in just ahead of them.

The woman immediately started asking him about Sasha and chatted with him as the line slowly progressed. When they reached the agent, he carefully looked at Noah's documents and then made some marks on the tickets. Noah thought he was past when the agent said, "Two tickets?"

Noah smiled as he cringed inside and said, "One for my dog. I like to have the whole first-class row. I know it's extravagant, but I can't travel without her." The agent saw the couple waiting and nodded. The woman waved and said, "Safe travels."

Noah had navigated the airport many times with his father and had even traveled to the Turks and Caicos Islands (TCI) several times. The boarding was uneventful, and he was thankful for the two first-class seats. The flight attendants chatted with him and admired Sasha. Once they got off the ground, the two of them curled up and slept blissfully, with Sasha on a blanket at his feet.

Passing through customs and immigration at the Provo airport turned into a much greater ordeal. The challenge was bringing a dog onto the island. Noah had researched the process and had all of the necessary paperwork, including the import permit, health and rabies certificates, paperwork stating Sasha was spayed (she wasn't), rabies testing, vaccinations, everything the websites said was needed. But the agent stopped him and said he must provide proof of training.

The agent was relentless and, at one point, actually threatened to euthanize Sasha. Seeing her reaction, Noah knew he needed to diffuse the situation. He said, "I understand your desire to keep problem pets off the island, but I'll bet you $1,000 Sasha can do any behavior you come up with in a two-minute span. If she fails, we'll get on the next flight to anywhere, and you get your money. If she passes, you agree she's trained and let us enter."

By now, a crowd of tourists had gathered, and the agent was feeling nervous. Tourism was a critical part of the economy. He said, "That won't be necessary, but I want her to sit, heel, speak, and stay. If she can do those commands, you can proceed."

Noah shook his head and said, "Sasha, sit please." Sasha sat down, crossed her front paws, and then looked over her shoulder at the agent. Noah wrinkled his nose and said a low "Don't." She uncrossed but wrinkled her nose back. The crowd burst out laughing.

Noah quickly went through the other behaviors and was rewarded with a round of applause from the other travelers. Sasha bowed down, and they roared with approval. The agent waved them away.

They walked out of the airport into the bright Caribbean sun. Noah said, "Good thing we didn't cause a scene. Let's get a cab."

The Ferry

Ruby, Ajax, and Avi walked to the pier where the Ferry stopped. She said their town was one of many small towns the Ferry stopped at along the coast. She didn't know their destination but understood Kellen had provided instructions.

The man working at the pier saw them walking up and said, "Hi Ruby. Whatcha got going on heah?" Avi smiled at his down-east accent, barely able to understand him. Before she could answer, he looked at Avi and said, "That's a cunnin' critta."

Ruby saved Avi by answering, "Jimmy, the girl and her dog need to take the Ferry. I can vouch for them. Let Hank know they're good people."

As the man nodded, he said, "Ferry's comin' in the hahba now." Ruby hugged Avi and then pulled back to look earnestly at Ajax.

"You take care of her, you hear? I sense you know everything I say, and I know you can do that."

She was only slightly surprised when Ajax lowered his head and gently pushed it against her leg in a display of gratitude and understanding. Avi could see her wipe away a tear as she turned away. Jimmy had already walked down the ramp to the dock and was helping tie the Ferry off. He said a few words to Captain Hank and then helped the one person who was getting off.

Jimmy held Avi's hand, and Hank helped her once she stepped onboard. The boat itself was relatively small, maybe 30 feet long. Seating was a series of benches on either side of the stern. The benches were covered but otherwise, the vessel was open to the elements. A middle-aged couple and a family with a boy about five years old were already seated.

Hank pulled away from the dock with the nonchalance that comes with years of experience. As they left the harbor, the wind picked up, making Avi shiver. Seeing her reaction, Hank reached into a bin and pulled out a thick wool blanket. Without a word, he handed it back to Avi, who nodded her appreciation and wrapped it around herself. Ajax leaned against her leg. The droning of the motor and the movement over the swells of the calm sea quickly put her to sleep.

Avi woke when the Ferry made its first and second stops. In both cases, someone came to meet them at the dock and took a mailbag from Hank. At the second stop, the couple also got off, smiling at Avi as they departed.

After the second stop, the family asked her a few questions, including Ajax's name. Avi answered as evasively as possible without raising suspicions. She didn't like how the little boy looked at Ajax, and Avi politely declined when the mother asked if it was okay if little Tommy could pet the dog.

Avi fell back to sleep and was jolted awake when Ajax let out a small yelp. Just after, Tommy yelled out, "He bit me. The bad dog bit me!"

As Hank slowed the boat, the father stood up and said, "We have to report that dog!" Standing up, he loomed over Avi as Ajax stood next to her, his ears back.

With the boat at a full stop and rolling slightly, Hank walked over as easily as if he were strolling down the sidewalk. Stepping between the man and Avi, he said in a low even voice, "Your boy poked the dog with the gaff." He pointed to a pole with a hook lying on the floor. "The dog never came close to your boy. I saw it."

As the mother exclaimed, "Tommy wouldn't do that!" the father attempted to stare down Hank. He said, "I'm taking that dog to the authorities. You'd better get out of my way." He started to reach out toward Hank.

"You touch me, and I'll throw you in the drink. You also better know how to swim, because you won't be coming back on this boat. As for the authorities, around here, I'm also known as Police Chief Hank. You just reported it. I have it from a credible witness, me, that you and your son are lying. Even if I didn't, your son has no bite marks. By the looks of that dog, if he bites, it's for keeps. Now, unless you want me to put the lot of you off at the next stop, sit down and be quiet."

Hank waited a moment until the man took a clumsy step back on the rolling deck. He walked back to the helm and got the Ferry moving again.

Only a few minutes later, the boat was pulling into the third port. Ajax jumped effortlessly over the gunwale and onto the dock. As Hank helped Avi step onto the small pier, he said, "I radioed ahead. They'll keep the general store open late for you. I suspect you may want to stop there to meet your ride. That's Tim." Hank pointed to the man who had taken the mailbag. "He'll help you."

As the Ferry pulled away, the father of the family called out, "You watch that dog." She then saw the boat steer into a wave that broke on the starboard side, spraying the family. She thought she saw a slight look of satisfaction on Hank's face.

Turning back to Tim, she saw the town. It looked like five houses, including the one with the General Store in the front. Looking down at Ajax, she could tell he was thinking the same thing. How did Kellen ever think to pick this place?

Walking over to the general store with Tim, she asked, "Where exactly are we?" He smiled and said, "Locals call this place Rose Point. You won't find it named as such on any map. People tend to come here to get away from something. We're not looking for so-called civilization to find us. It's a tight-knit group if you're accepted. The woman over there is Ann. She's Hank's wife. You're in good hands."

Ann introduced herself to Avi and nodded to Ajax before bringing them into the store. Like Hank, Ann was a woman of few words who kept her emotions in check. There was already a pile of clothes on the counter, which Avi confirmed were her size. Ann suggested, "You might want to pick up some candy or other things. We don't keep much like that at the house and won't be back down here for a week or two." Looking at Ajax, she gave a slight smile, "Same goes for you. I think there's elk antlers in the back." She only raised her eyebrow slightly when he trotted back, picked one out, and brought it back to the counter.

When they went back out, Avi looked for Ann's vehicle. Instead, the woman walked back down the dock where a small Boston Whaler skiff was tied off. The woman stepped in and then held out a hand. Avi stepped in, followed by Ajax. Moments later, they were cruising up the coast in the dark, Ann seeming to know the way by heart.

Providenciales, TCI

Getting a cab in front of the airport had never been a problem when Noah was with his father. Standing there with Sasha, however, every driver said, "No dogs!" Finally, he tipped a porter several dollars to help find one who would take them across the island. When they saw the car, Sasha was apprehensive. It didn't have any indications it was a cab. Noah shook his head in frustration. It had taken almost an hour to get a ride.

The driver came over and asked, "Where to?" Noah told him he wanted to go to a popular shopping area on the other side of the island. "No problem." The man had the easy- going attitude Noah admired about the TCI residents. Looking at Sasha, she indicated the driver was trustworthy.

As they drove, the driver asked Noah a couple of questions but quickly sensed he didn't want to talk about his visit to the island. When his cellphone rang, the man took the call and got a serious look. He asked a couple of inaudible questions. Finally, he glanced at Noah. "My wife has an issue at our house. It's only a little out of the way. She really needs me."

Noah looked to Sasha, who indicated no bad intent, and replied, "Of course." After ten minutes, they pulled off the main road. The house they stopped at was well kept and had a small table in the shade where a girl appeared to be doing homework.

The man said, "Jenny, would you get this young man and his dog a drink while I go help your grandmother?" Jenny nodded shyly and ran inside. Coming back outside, she handed Noah a glass of water and put a bowl of water down for Sasha.

As they took the drinks, Noah said, "Thank you, Jenny. My name's Noah, and this is Sasha." Sasha did a little bow to Jenny's delight.

She said, "I'm sorry you had to come here. My grandmother was having problems with the washer, and it started to leak really bad."

Noah smiled and replied, "That's okay. What are you working on?"

Jenny showed him her math homework and explained the questions. Noah had thought he might be able to help, but the younger girl was extremely bright and was having no difficulty with the problems. Finally, she cut to the chase and said, "Can I pet Sasha?" Before Noah could answer, Sasha laid her head against Jenny's hand.

The ice broken, Jenny and Noah talked about life on the island, Sasha, their schools, and Noah's life at home. Sasha lay between them, allowing Jenny to stroke her fur. Jenny had just asked Noah what brought him to the island when her grandfather came back out.

Smiling at the girl affectionately, her grandfather said, "Jenny would you go in to help Grandma for a minute? I need a word with this young man."

After she left, the man held out his hand. "I'm John. My wife is Leah. I overheard you say your name's Noah, and the dog is Sasha." Noah nodded, and John continued, "I'm pretty good at reading people. I sense you may be in trouble. Can we help?"

Noah looked to Sasha, who indicated the man's concern was genuine. "I don't want you to know too much because it could be bad for you. But as you guessed, we're in trouble.

People are trying to catch us to force my dad to do things he doesn't want to do. We came here to get away. A couple of years ago, I met someone at the Ports of Call when we were here on vacation. I think he can help us. He has a small inn on one of the other islands. I don't think the people will find us there."

John nodded, "That might work, but I think I have something better if you're interested. My brother on North Caicos has a little apartment attached to his house. He teaches at the school, so you could attend it and blend right in. He and his wife like dogs, so Sasha shouldn't be a problem."

Noah looked to Sasha, thought for a few moments, and then said, "Thank you so much, John. We'll do it."

An Undisclosed Location

Professor Anderson looked around his bare room. Without a clock, he had lost track of how long he had been there but estimated it had been three days. Their captors seemed to want to leave them in isolation. Food and water had been slid through a slot in the door at regular intervals. Otherwise, there had been no contact since arrival.

He had learned Indira was in the next cell and was unhurt by tapping out messages using the slow but effective 5x5 prison tap code. They had used this method previously in their offices, sending messages like "Call" (3, 1, pause, 1, 1, pause, 1, 3, pause, 1, 3) to cut off unwanted visitors. His adrenaline spiked when he suddenly heard her tap out, "Here."

He had only moments to gain his composure before his door opened and his captor looked into the cell. "You. Come with me." Nodding, he stepped through the doorway and got his first look outside his cell/room. If the gray hallway was any indication, this was a pretty cheerless place. As they turned a corner, he saw Indira ahead of him.

They were escorted into a room with a conference table. A large video screen was at the end, and Seven (with his face blacked out) was already visible. Other than electronic equipment, the room itself was utterly characterless. Even without access to makeup or a shower, Indira looked composed and professional.

"Professors Verma and Anderson, welcome to your temporary accommodations. My apologies that they're so uninteresting. I assure you it is only necessary until we have our other facilities ready."

Indira cut him off, "Where are our children? I don't know what you think we'll do for you, but I won't do anything until I know Avi and Noah are safe."

"Your children are fine. They've both left the area per whatever plan you put in place with them. We've tracked them loosely but have no intention of trying to find them as long as you cooperate. We aren't running a daycare center here."

"And what of Kellen and the dogs?" Jens glanced at Indira as he said it. "Are they okay as well?"

"The dogs are with the children. However, Dr. Jackson," Seven continued after a hesitation, "had a mishap that has resulted in extensive hospital time. I think you should take his situation as a lesson that it's better to cooperate than to attempt to thwart us."

"And why should we do that? What assurances do you give? Will you ever let us go? Leave us alone?" Indira showed a rare burst of frustration.

"We have no intention of keeping you forever. We only want to learn what's necessary to be able to share your research. If you hadn't falsified your lab work, we wouldn't have needed to go to these extremes. It's you who keep forcing these situations to become contentious." A slight edge had crept into Seven's smooth voice.

Jens started to speak, and Seven put his hand up, cutting him off. "I'm not here to discuss or negotiate. I just thought you deserved to know the situation. In three weeks, your new lab will be ready. It's in a remote area and you will be transported there. Meanwhile, we will provide you with assistants and anything you need."

"What about access to the internet? Or e-mail?" Indira raised her eyebrow. "We sometimes need input from our colleagues."

"You'll have indirect access through your assistants. I've asked my colleagues to provide you with your laptops, albeit without internet access. You'll have them tomorrow, and I'm hoping you'll start laying out a transition plan. For now, I suggest you rest."

The professors were led out of the room but did not return to their previous cells. Instead, they were brought into a small suite containing a common area with a kitchen, a table, and a video screen displaying an outdoor scene. There were two desks at each end of the room next to doors leading to separate bedrooms. Each bedroom had a bathroom with a shower and a smaller video screen streaming the same outdoor scene. In the corner of the screen was a small clock showing the time.

Indira went into the kitchen and started preparing coffee. "I'm dying for this. I think we need to make a plan."

Jens nodded. "Please make mine extra strong. We will need it."

Defense Research Intelligence Agency (DRIA)

Director Johnston reviewed the reports for the missing children and the two professors. So far, no solid leads, even though he had his two best teams, six agents total, working full-time to determine what had happened to them. He was pondering his next steps when his assistant, Cindy, tapped on his door.

"Director Johnston? General Clayton has asked to see you. I indicated you could be in his office in ten minutes. Is that acceptable?"

Johnston nodded and collected his reports to discuss with the General. The Protectors program was a sensitive subject right now, and the apparent loss of not just their research, but also all of the key scientists, were topics they would most likely be reviewing.

He was shown right in to see the General. He turned down the coffee and water offered to him by the General's assistant and waited until the door was shut before speaking. "What can I do for you?"

The General turned and gestured toward a seat at his large table. "Michael, please sit. We need to discuss this whole Protectors situation."

"Stephen, we have our finest men and women on this. We're going to figure out what happened to them. We'll get them and our research back."

The General wiped his brow and sighed, "See, that's the thing. It's not clear to anyone the scientists themselves didn't just stage all of this. I mean, the kids are definitely on the run."

Johnston started to interject, but the General held up a finger stopping him.

"This has been reviewed at levels well above this office. I'm being told we're chasing a wild goose. You need to let this one go."

"General, with all due respect. We know a separatist group penetrated our organization. The labs were ransacked. We need to follow this through."

The General crossed his arms, "Those Separatist Northwest folks don't have the resources to do what you're suggesting. Look at their two failed attempts to get the kids. Then they shoot the other guy while trying to get him? I'm telling you, the researchers staged this, and you're playing the fool. Stop it NOW!"

Before Johnston could make another plea, the General turned away. Shaking his head, Johnston walked back to his desk dismayed.

Seven's Office

Seven had promised the Chairman he would provide an update after speaking with the professors. He wasn't relishing the prospect of reporting failure to apprehend the children. His only hope was that his approach with the professors would be considered an acceptable alternative to capturing the children. Sighing, he clicked the link, and the chatbox opened.

Chairman: Report.

Seven: We have "conditioned" the professors per our plan and have had a successful discussion with them.

Chairman: What about the children and dogs?

Seven: Each child is traveling with a dog. Surprisingly, they have managed to elude us. We have camera footage from the airport security feed. The boy and his dog were near a gate for a flight to the Turks and Caicos Islands. We're searching all lodging possibilities and should find him soon.

Chairman: And the girl?

Seven: She's more problematic. We have traffic footage near the park showing her and Ajax in a car traveling north. We weren't able to track the vehicle. We believe the driver used secondary roads.

Chairman: And the professors' reactions?

Seven: We told them we're not trying to capture the children. The professors recognize we have the resources to find their children and the dogs. We told them we are not trying since we don't want the burden of caring for them.

Chairman: Probability of success?

Seven: My estimate is 70% probability they'll cooperate without finding the children. We will continue to seek them at a low level.

Chairman: That is not acceptable. We have provided considerable resources, and yet you continue to struggle. Find a way to improve this probability, or your successor will.

Seven: I understand.

Seven severed the link and closed his eyes. So typical. Upper management had no understanding or appreciation of the challenges at the operations level. He knew the "severance package" in the Faction was harsh. He needed to find a way to make this work.

The Coast of Maine

Hank and Ann's place was a ten-minute boat ride or 25-minute ATV ride into the village. Avi marveled at the harsh beauty of the area and the fantastic views their compact house had since it was perched on a cliff overlooking the ocean. She enjoyed walking and running with Ajax on the various paths along the shore the couple had carved out over the years.

Food was mostly items from the couple's extensive garden supplemented by fish and lobster Hank received in trade for their vegetables. Avi volunteered to help anytime she could, and Ann taught her about preserving food, the weather, and generally how to live away from civilization.

Avi was surprised when she found out most of the appliances, including the refrigerator and lights, were powered by propane. The small amount of electricity used was produced primarily from solar panels on the roof, but there was also a propane generator for the long, dark winter months.

Rainy days and evenings were spent by the woodstove reading the many classic books the couple had in their library. Avi and Ajax also had significant time alone while Ann was off visiting other families and Hank was piloting the ferry. They put this time to use by practicing Kellen's sign language.

The two things Avi could never figure out were why the couple lived this solitary life and how they could have met Kellen. She asked Ann about it shortly after arriving. Ann got up, seemed to think for a minute, and replied, "Some things are best left in the past."

Hank was even less communicative. He would take Avi and Ajax out in the skiff to fish, or would walk with them on the paths, but said little. He was always kind and had a deep calm about him. Even though she felt safe, one day she asked him what would happen if the men chasing her found them here.

"Not many people come here. An occasional tourist arrives in the summer and sometimes in the early fall. The only reasonable way to reach the area is by the ferry, seaplane, or helicopter. In all cases, you have to stop in the village first. No one comes to these parts without me knowing."

Looking at Ajax, Hank continued, "Plus, something tells me that dog might have a thing or two to say about it. Can't even come into the boat without him tagging along." Ajax gave the man a look. Even with the doggy life vest he was wearing, the boat made him nervous.

As the ten-day prescribed check-in approached, Avi thought she might have to go back to the village to get access to the outside world. She explained the situation to Ann and was surprised when the older woman took her to Hank's desk. Pulling a laptop out from one of the drawers, Ann explained they had recently purchased it. "We thought you might eventually need it."

The bigger surprise was the computer already had privacy software set up and had internet access via their satellite Wi-Fi. Avi was incredulous. "You guys have had internet this whole time and haven't told me?"

"Well, Dear, we felt this place is best understood without the distractions of the outside world. Plus, we think it's safer for you to stay off the internet."

Avi nodded, "You know, it has been like having a vacation from my worries. But now I want to know what's happening with my mom and my friends."

North Caicos

Like most tourists visiting TCI, Noah had spent most of his previous visits in plush resorts or on well-organized excursions. He had never been to the less populated islands like North Caicos. While he had always found the islands beautiful, living with a local family helped him see it in a whole new light.

John's brother, James, had allowed them to move into a small but charming apartment connected to his home. Noah and Sasha ate with the family, went to school together during the day, and helped with chores in the afternoons and evenings.

James and his wife, Dinah, had five children, all of whom were grown, but there seemed to be an endless number of grandchildren who visited regularly. Two of them, Matthew and Sarah, were close to Noah in age and attended school with him. They both adored Sasha and would invite her and Noah to swim and play with them and their friends after school.

As the check-in approached, Noah asked them about getting access to a computer and the internet. Sarah said it was not a problem. Her family had a desktop that he could borrow. They could check it out after school. Noah told her that he would require access tomorrow. His calls were at 3:00 pm, but he would need to download some software first. Sarah raised an eyebrow, but Noah assured her it wouldn't hurt anything.

The next day Sarah brought them to her home. The computer was in a hutch in the corner of the kitchen. Noah inserted the thumb drive that downloaded the conferencing software Diego had developed. It wasn't sophisticated, and only allowed text transfer and file uploads, but everything passing through was heavily encrypted.

At exactly 3:00, he launched the code.

NOAH → Here

ALEX → Here

AVI → Here

Noah felt a surge of adrenaline. They had only briefly tested the software, but his real worry was Avi and Alex might not be available to join. Knowing they were both safe, at least for now, was a huge relief.

NOAH → All ok here. Avi?

AVI → All ok here also. Alex, news from home?

ALEX → Kellen is doing much better. Under tight security. Should be home in a week.

AVI → Alex, update on our parents?

ALEX → Still missing. Kellen says DRIA is searching, but no leads.

Sasha was watching the screen closely and was visibly relieved when she read Kellen was better. When she saw the professors were still missing, a thought came to her mind. As she communicated the idea to Noah, he became excited and exclaimed, "Awesome! I hope Avi can ask Ajax."

NOAH → Avi, would Ajax have insight about our parents' location?

There was a pause as Avi and Ajax conferred. Noah feared their ability to communicate would limit Ajax's response, so he was pleasantly surprised at her reply.

AVI → Ajax may have a lead! We will work on it and get back to you tomorrow.

NOAH → Alex, we may need Diego's help. Could you check on his availability?

ALEX → Will do! I will bring him tomorrow.

NOAH → Same time tomorrow. Out.

Noah looked at Sasha and smiled. "Good idea to ask Ajax! If he can find a location, Diego will be able to research it." Sasha did a little dance and then stopped. Her question was on Noah's mind as well. Then what do we do?

The Coast of Maine

Avi's original question to Ajax was, "Do you think you can help us find our parents?" His response was an immediate yes, but she realized she hadn't asked the right question. "Do you know where our parents are being held?"

After considering, his response was less confident, but still yes. Avi was so excited she hugged him before responding to Noah and Alex. Ajax did his equivalent of blushing as she typed. She rolled her eyes, "Sorry, I know that was a bit much."

After signing off, she said, "Okay, let's figure this out. We know where I first met you. But that warehouse was abandoned when the police searched it."

Ajax signed he had been brought to another facility. Avi realized it was the one he had been in when he escaped. He indicated he traveled from there to the University.

"Can you show me on the map where the facility was?" She understood his answer as "approximately." After Avi accessed the map, Ajax quickly directed her to focus on the western part of Massachusetts and southern Vermont. Working together, they were able to track back on the roads he followed to come home. Even though the travel had been primarily through small towns, Avi marveled he had been able to find his way. When she asked Ajax how it was possible, she interpreted his answer as "instinct."

Finally, after several hours of searching and examining multiple locations using Google Earth, Avi located a group of buildings Ajax immediately acknowledged as the correct location. It was in a wooded area by itself and appeared to consist of three reasonably large buildings.

Avi noted the GPS coordinates. Zooming in on one of the images, she could see the name "Assigned Process Sensors" on the main building. When she completed a search on this name, she found a website. When she navigated to it, it only displayed a company name and "Under Construction."

She smiled at Ajax. "We're close! Time to bring in the big guns. Diego will be able to figure out who these people are." Ajax thumped his tail. It was a good day's work.

An Undisclosed Location

Seven reviewed the research plan and various requests submitted by the two professors. It was thorough and reasonably consistent with what they were already building in the new facility. He noted the additions and e-mailed a request to the project manager. Within an hour, she responded to his message.

> Seven,
>
> These are minor changes but will add about three days to the overall timeline. Additional cost is $250,000. I've attached the cost breakdown and revised Gantt chart. The bottom line is the facility will be ready in ten days if you approve revisions.
>
> Kate

Seven looked through the revised documents. As usual, Kate was thorough and efficient. He felt they were vulnerable holding the professors at this site, but the more significant issue was they couldn't get the research started until they were in the new facility.

Kate,

The revisions are approved. We appreciate your quick response. Please proceed.

Seven

Glancing at the clock, Seven realized it was almost time for his update with the Chairman. Kate's revised plan was just in time to add to the discussion. He wrote a reminder to have his secretary send a nice bottle of wine to express his appreciation. Clicking on the link, he initiated the chat.

Chairman: Report.

Seven: We have made substantial progress this week. The professors have developed a research plan and appear to be cooperating.

Chairman: Do you think the plan is executable?

Seven: Our science team has reviewed it with the professors. It addresses the gaps we have been encountering in genetics and behavioral development.

Chairman: Do you have the resources needed?

Seven: The new facility should be ready in two weeks. Additional costs to accommodate the professors' demands should not exceed $500,000.

Chairman: How soon will we know we have success?

Seven: According to the professors, they realized Ajax was a success about two months after birth. Add in 30 days to prepare, and a little over two months of gestation.

Chairman: So, 5 to 6 months from now?

Seven: Yes, but keep in mind the subject will still be a puppy at that time.

Chairman: Of course. The children?

Seven: We have tracked the boy to the Turks and Caicos Islands. We have checked all possible lodging but have not found him. I have sent a resource to search locally.

Chairman: The girl?

Seven: We've still not found her. Her mother does not appear to know where she went. I have a suspicion Dr. Jackson knows.

Chairman: Let's not pursue her for now. Focus on executing the professors' plan.

Seven: Understood.

Seven smiled as he signed off. Telling the Chairman a higher budget and longer timeline virtually guaranteed his ability to deliver the project early and under cost. All of the pieces were falling into place.

Alex's House

When Alex explained Noah and Avi needed his help, Diego's immediate response was, "Of course!" Neither boy knew the details of the problem or who was involved. They just knew their friends needed them.

At exactly 3:00 pm the following day, Alex launched the code to establish the session. He waited for Noah and Avi to join before announcing he was present with Diego.

NOAH→ Here

AVI → Here

ALEX → Here with Diego.

NOAH → Excellent. Avi, any update?

AVI → YES! Ajax was able to trace his way back to the facility. The GPS coordinates are: 42.34685, -72.26249

NOAH → Is there anything there?

AVI → Google Earth shows a company called Assigned Process Sensors. Website exists, but no information.

NOAH → Multi-prong attack. Avi, see if Ajax can describe the buildings and what's in them.

AVI → He thinks he can.

NOAH → Diego, find out everything you can about Assigned Process Sensors. Also, I need you to work up a Jax.

Alex looked to Diego. "What's a Jax?"

Diego smiled. "Do you remember that guy, Jax, who picked on us every time we went to get pizza?" Alex nodded. "Did you ever notice how all of a sudden he quit doing it?" Alex raised his eyebrow. "Well, Noah got sick of his crap and decided to do something about it. We set up a camera and planted a bug in his dorm room. We caught him paying off a teaching assistant to give him answers to his tests. We got a video of the TA visiting and audio of them discussing it."

Alex shook his head in disbelief. "You extorted a guy for picking on you 12's?"

Diego smiled. "We like to think of it as guiding him to a righteous path. We told him to stop the bullying and the cheating. He's a better man for it. What Noah is asking for is research on the company and surveillance on the site."

Alex turned back to the computer.

ALEX → Diego is good to go, anything for me?

NOAH → Can you travel to the location?

ALEX → Pretty sure I can get a ride. What will I do?

NOAH → Confirm you can. Let's discuss tomorrow. Same time.

As he turned off the text conference, Alex could see Diego already starting his search on the company. Without looking up, he asked Alex, "Who are you thinking to give you a ride?"

Alex thought only for a second before he said, "Principal Banks."

Diego smiled, "This is going to be fun."

The Coast of Maine

Avi turned to Ajax after completing the conference. "So, how are we going to map out the buildings?" Ajax gave his signal to go out. Avi walked outside with him and followed him to a sandy area behind the home. Ajax used his paw to mark out three spots. As he signed to her, Avi caught on this was the layout of the site. She quickly sketched out a representation of the buildings using a drawing program on the laptop.

Stepping on one of the marks, Ajax signed, "Empty." Avi noted this on her sketch. Stepping on another, he signed what she interpreted as, "Storage." Then, as he stepped to the third, Avi said, "So that's the main building."

Grabbing a stick in his mouth, Ajax drew a pretty good representation of the building in the sand. He was able to sketch out the general layout, including a reception area, the office area, and the rooms where he slept and trained. He was also able to put in the halls and the doors and the location of security guards. Together, they determined the location of the ten security cameras used to monitor the site.

When Avi finished transcribing the layout, Ajax reviewed the drawing on the laptop. It was as he remembered. He was also able to communicate there were two guards during the day and four at night.

Avi saved her notes and sat next to Ajax. As the two of them looked out over the ocean, she felt a pang of loneliness. Ajax leaned into her, and she smiled as she heard Ann calling out, "Avi, Ajax, supper's on the table!"

The Academy

The next morning Alex skipped his second-period gym class and went to Principal Bank's office. After he waited just a few minutes, she came out to see him.

"Good morning, Alex. What can I do for you?"

"Good morning, Principal Banks. Can we speak privately?"

"Of course, please come into my office."

Once in the office, Alex closed the door and took a seat across from her. He turned slightly so her nosy assistant, Joshua, could only see his back. She raised her eyebrow, "Is all this necessary? Joshua can't hear us."

Alex looked into her eyes and said, "It's Avi and Noah. They need our help." He briefly outlined what little he knew. He finished with, "We think we know who's been chasing them. We've identified a location where these people may be holding Avi and Noah's parents."

"Well, then we have to tell the police and the DRIA. They'll know what to do."

Alex shook his head, "We don't trust them. The man who came here posing as an agent had just been discovered as an infiltrator of the DRIA. We also know some members of the police have been compromised. All we want to do for now is check out this lead. And I know I can trust you to help me."

"What are you asking me to do, Alex?"

"Would you drive me out to the location? The plan is to plant a surveillance camera to see who comes and goes. Trees surround the site, so it should be pretty easy. Noah also wants a listening device placed in the reception area."

Groaning, she said, "I must be crazy to consider this, but I do realize the seriousness of the situation and the need for discretion. When would we do it?"

"Tomorrow afternoon and evening. I need to think of a reason to get onto the property in the afternoon, and then I'll plant the camera tomorrow night. It's about a 90-minute drive."

She nodded and said, "Okay. I'll do it. I can also get us into the building. I still do some sales work for a grounds-keeping company. I'll do a cold call and leave pamphlets and a card."

"Awesome! Thank you! I'll let you know the details as soon as I can." He got up and smiled. "One last thing, can you please give me a hall pass, so I can go see Diego?"

Diego was working in the technology lab, where he spent all of his free time. Hearing Alex walk in, he looked up from the contraption he was working on and smiled. To

Alex, it looked like one of those plug-in air fresheners.

"What've you got there, Diego?"

"These are the devices we'll plant in the reception area. They started their lives as air fresheners, but I've converted them into transmitters. They run off AC power and connect to the guest Wi-Fi. I've already established they have Xfinity, so they'll automatically connect. Every two hours, they'll post audio files to a website I've set up. I have a program that automatically downloads the files and screens out periods of inactivity and background noise."

Alex frowned. "Do you think we'll hear anything worthwhile in the reception area?"

"My guess is Noah wants to hear conversations between the guards. In off-hours, they'll be pretty lax. When you plant these, just plug them close to where you think the guards will hang out talking. I think it's a long shot, but worth trying."

Alex nodded. "How about the camera?"

Diego got even more excited. "I got these online and only had to make minor modifications. They're solar-powered, use cellular communication, and are well camouflaged." He turned one on and then held up his tablet. The image from the camera showed on the tablet.

Alex said, "Wow! But won't it be hard to watch the feed all day?"

"That's the sweet part. The devices have motion sensors and only turn on and transmit if they are activated. We can turn them on remotely or allow the sensors to trigger them. The video is also backed up for 48 hours."

Diego pulled out some straps. "Each camera can be mounted on any surface using these camo straps. It takes about one minute to mount, turn on, and confirm they're working."

Alex examined the camera and started smiling. "Diego, yahr wicked smaht!" Diego laughed at the exaggerated New England accent and jargon.

As Alex practiced turning the camera on and checking the feed from his cell phone, Diego said, "I also researched Assigned Process Sensors. They're an LLC owned by a shell company incorporated in the Caymans. I can dig further, but I suspect it would set off flags. It doesn't appear they've sold anything yet. But the most intriguing thing is they also own property in northwest Ohio."

"Diego, I take it back. You're way beyond 'wicked smaht.' I can't wait to tell Noah and Avi."

North Caicos

Noah got in position and looked over his notes. His first objective was to get his dad and Avi's mom back. After that, he wanted to disable the group holding them. But, first things first. He looked over the critical tasks he had jotted down on his notepad:

OBJECTIVE: Get our folks back
STEPS:
- Enable surveillance of the known location
    - Provide layout of buildings (Ajax, Avi)
    - Provide equipment for use in surveillance (Diego)
    - Put equipment in place (Alex, TBD?)
- Identify the organization and additional locations
    - Provide info on the organization (Diego)
- Develop the rest of the plan
    - Steps TBD based on information gathered

The other students in his leadership class picked on him for laying out simple summaries like this, but it helped him to see the plan. He saw Sasha looking at the list. Thumping her tail, she provided her support.

Knowing how he wanted the meeting to progress, he initiated the conference.

NOAH→ Here

AVI → Here

ALEX → Here with Diego and Principal Banks.

Noah balked when he saw Principal Banks' name on the screen.

NOAH → Banks??? Too much risk for her?

ALEX → She understands. She's ready to help.

Sasha seemed to agree with Alex. Noah asked Sasha, "Are you sure she can be trusted? What if she decides to go to the police or DRIA?" Seeing Sasha's reaction, Noah had to agree, "You're right. It's too late to second guess this now."

NOAH → Avi, progress on the layout?

AVI → Layout is uploaded. Note position of front door & reception including coffee area.

ALEX → Diego asks if a device should be located near coffee?

AVI → Affirmative. Ajax says the guards meet there before a shift to discuss issues.

NOAH → Perfect. Put both devices in this area. External cameras?

AVI → Wooded area allows close approach. Near edge provides adequate light.

ALEX → Diego confirms this should work.

NOAH → Alex, transportation?

ALEX → Principal Banks is assisting. Tomorrow evening is a go.

NOAH → Diego, any progress on the organization?

ALEX → Diego says early stages. Key finding is a second location. Details attached.

AVI → This is huge. Will discuss with Ajax.

NOAH → Excellent progress. Reconvene in two days to discuss outcome. Same time.

Noah looked over the layout Avi had provided. Smiling at Sasha, he said, "Ajax is really something. This is going to be a huge help." Seeing her response, he playfully said, "Someone's got a crush on Ajax!" Her playful nip got him back on task.

Opening Diego's file, he was most interested in the second site. Putting the GPS coordinates into Google Earth, he saw what appeared to be new construction. The date on the image was only two weeks earlier. "Sasha, this is it! This is the new research facility."

The Coast of Maine – Ann and Hank's House

Like Noah, Avi was researching the second facility owned by Assigned Process Sensors. She asked Ajax if he knew anything that might give them a clue about the location. He was attempting to answer when they heard a boat approaching. Looking down, she saw Hank pulling up to the dock. Through the window, she saw Ann walking out to greet Hank. It was all normal, except someone was in the skiff with him.

Avi sprinted down to the dock but was still several steps slower than Ajax. She laughed out loud as Kellen dropped to his knees and took the dog into his arms. As she reached them, she felt Kellen draw her in as well. The massive three-way hug was breathtaking. As she felt the tears on her cheeks, she noticed Kellen was crying, too.

As Hank walked by, he said, "Well, c'mon you three. I suspect Ann has supper waiting." His face looked mostly expressionless, but Avi thought she detected a twinkle in his eye.

Over dinner, Kellen recounted his ordeal. Fortunately, the bullet had missed all vital organs, but he had lost a significant amount of blood. Even with the EMTs working feverishly, his blood pressure was dangerously low when they reached the emergency room. He didn't recall anything from the first few days in the hospital. After that, it was just a slow recovery.

The police had been very diligent at first and posted a guard outside his room. As Kellen recovered and the days went by, they became lax. When he was released to go home, they decided a patrol car checking on the house once every hour or so would be adequate.

A couple of evenings later, he walked into his kitchen and found two men sitting at his table. The tension in Kellen's voice increased as he described the situation.

"They graciously asked me to join them at my own table. Two guns were lying in plain sight in case I needed persuasion. I sat and asked them what they wanted. They asked me about you two." He nodded at Avi and Ajax. "Nothing about Noah and Sasha. Nothing about the professors."

Avi said in a low tone, "We're pretty sure they have our folks. I can't believe the police didn't tell you that. I'm in touch with Noah. We're going to find them and set them free."

Kellen nodded and continued, "Well, I jumped up and hit both of them in the face with the table. I was out the door before the scumbags could grab their guns. Fortunately, I still had my wallet and phone. It took me the better part of a day to get to the ferry, but I made it here."

"I'm concerned they didn't ask me about Noah. They clearly know he's not with you." Kellen paused to ponder over another bite of cobbler.

Hank spoke up for the first time that evening, "I'd bet they are closing in on the boy and the other dog. I think it's time you get them up here."

North Caicos

James knocked on Noah's door lightly. When Noah invited him in, James responded, "I think you better come over to the house."

As Noah walked up, both hosts were looking concerned. Dinah held up her phone and showed Noah a picture of a man in a golf shirt and sport coat. "Do you know this man?"

Noah looked closely and looked to Sasha. "No. Should I?"

"Over on Provo, he's been asking if anyone has seen a boy and a white dog. My understanding is you tried to get to the Ports of Call shopping center. That's where he was when my friend took this picture."

Noah looked down at Sasha before asking, "Do you think he'll find us?"

Dinah said, "I think he knows you're here. I asked my friend who works down by the ferry dock to keep an eye out for strangers. Two men arrived an hour ago. North Caicos is still a small place. They'll find you soon."

As Noah's eyes went wide, James held his hands out in a calming gesture. "Matt is down at the dock. Sarah will be here in a minute to take you over to the boat. We can get you to the airport in time for the next flight out. But you'll need to get a ticket."

Noah ran back to his room. Before collecting his stuff, he powered up the disposable phone he had brought for emergencies. He quickly texted Alex, the only person who had all of the information for his false identity.

N: Need a ticket home on next flight out of Provo, TCI.

As he packed, he urged the phone to show a response. After what seemed like hours, but was only a minute, the reply came.

A: On it. Kellen had said you might be in trouble.

N: You're in touch with Kellen?

A: He and Avi are together. Stay tuned.

N: Out. Later.

Grabbing his bag, he was surprised to see Sarah pulling up in a golf cart. He hugged Dinah and James as he got in and thanked them. James put his hand on Sasha's shoulder as Dinah said, "God be with you."

Sarah drove down the main road toward the dock. As they passed by a side road, a car suddenly came out. The car clipped the cart's rear bumper, turning it and flipping it over onto its side. Sasha managed to jump clear, but Noah and Sarah, buckled in, were momentarily stuck inside.

A man jumped out of the car, said something into a radio, and then walked over to the cart. He pulled a knife and reached in to cut the seat belt off Noah. In full fury, Sasha jumped up onto the overturned cart, touching it just once before landing on the man's neck and chest. Her momentum carried her past him, and she pivoted to go back at him. She paused when she heard a deep male voice say, "What's all this going on?"

Sarah called out. "Help us!"

Their assailant growled, "I'm just here for the boy and the dog. The rest of you just get out of here."

"I guess we aren't going to do that." The man with the deep voice stepped into view. The assailant attempted to reach his knife but was cut short when a huge fist smashed into his face. He fell to the ground motionless.

After Noah finished extracting himself and Sarah from the cart, he looked over at the massive man who had helped them. Before he could speak, Sarah said, "Thank you, Tiny! Can you make sure that man is detained for a while?"

"Oh, I don't think he's going anywhere soon." He walked over and easily righted the cart.

Noah looked at the damage to the cart. "I'm so sorry."

Sarah waved him off. "Don't worry about it. It can be fixed. Let's go."

They were close enough to run the rest of the way to the dock where Matt was preparing to cast off in a small runabout boat. Sasha gave Noah a look. He said, "Please. There's no other way right now." Gingerly climbing on, she curled up in the back of the boat.

As they pulled away from the dock, they heard another boat coming from further down the island. The runabout sped up as Matt pushed it to its limits, but the other vessel with its multiple outboard motors gained quickly. Reaching an area where there were many small islands and channels, Matt attempted to shake the larger, faster pursuer.

In an open bay, the bigger boat pulled alongside, and the man grinned at Matt. Noah was surprised when Matt smiled back and then suddenly turned into a small opening. The larger boat continued by and was momentarily left behind. Rather than pushing his advantage, Matt slowed the runabout down.

"What are you doing?" Noah was wide-eyed. He looked back at Sasha, who was not enjoying any of this.

Matt glanced over his shoulder to watch for the pursuer. "We have a secret. I think our friend is in for a surprise."

When the faster boat came into view, Matt gunned it. The runabout sprinted through the channel, barely ten feet wide, with ease. The larger vessel's pilot had trouble following but quickly caught up when they entered a wide bay. As Matt shot through another small opening, he winked at Noah.

The other boat's engines made a sudden roar as the props were knocked up and out of the water. Matt slowed down, and they turned back to see the larger boat taking on water. The pursuer's motionless body had been thrown clear and was lying on the bank.

Matt said to Noah, "Should we go get him?"

"No. But we should let someone know he's here. What happened?"

"This is a jet boat. I also know this area extremely well. My cousin and I give tours through here to tourists looking for a place to get away for the day. There's a rock between those two Cays. We made it over. Barely. He didn't."

The Airport

Matt dropped Noah at a dock not too far from the airport. John was there waiting. As Matt pulled in, John helped him tie off the runabout. Matt quickly explained what had happened with both the golf cart and the other boat. John looked concerned and promised to report it to the authorities.

Hugging Noah and Sasha, Matt said, "It's been an adventure meeting you. Promise me you'll come back."

Noah smiled, "You know we will. I love this place. You guys are like family to me. Plus, you all have to come to New England and visit me!"

Driving the short distance to the airport was thankfully uneventful. As Sasha hopped out, she pointed to a man near the car and signaled, "Bad intent."

Noah signaled John, who walked over to the man. "I haven't seen you around here. Can I help you?" Looking down at the phone in the man's hand, he saw him creating a text, "THEY ARE H." Grabbing the phone, John signaled a police officer as the man protested.

As the officer approached, the man said, "He stole my phone!"

The officer addressed John. "What's going on, John?"

"This man is up to no good. Could you detain him? And by the way, I think his cell phone is about to be accidentally destroyed."

The officer nodded. "Got it, John. Come with me, Sir." The man protested as he was led away.

"Noah. Be careful. My guess is he's not the only one watching."

"John, I can't thank you enough." They hugged, and John knelt and looked in Sasha's eyes, then he whispered in her ear.

At the counter, Noah picked up the two first-class tickets Alex had purchased. He was expecting to see he'd be on a flight to Miami then Boston. To his surprise, in Miami he would transfer to a flight to Bangor, Maine. He signed to Sasha, "Off we go," and she signed back, "No boats, please!"

On the Road, Western Massachusetts

Alex placed the package from Diego into the back of Principal Bank's SUV. Next, he added a compound bow, a quiver full of arrows, and camouflage coveralls. The principal gave him a questioning look.

"The best way for me to set up the cameras is to go in on foot. I confirmed the site borders on conservation land that is currently open for hunting season with the appropriate permit." He pointed to his head. "I did pick up a thing or two at your esteemed learning establishment."

She shook her head. "Keep up the wisecracks, and this will be a long ride for you sitting in the way, way back."

Alex smiled. He was a bit apprehensive about spending several hours in the car with her. They had a good relationship, but she still was his principal. A little levity would help the miles go by quicker.

Looking in the back seat, he saw a bunch of pamphlets for a landscaping company. It was his turn to give a questioning look.

"I need some way to get into the building. As I mentioned earlier, I help my cousin by doing sales work for his company. Making cold calls to facilities like this is pretty typical. The cover story is we're considering expanding west."

Alex asked, "What if they call your cousin?"

"He'll give them a bid. He's considering buying a small company near where we're going. I told him I might stop into a place or two while I'm out here."

Alex relaxed and let the miles roll by. It turned out Principal Banks was a great traveling companion and would chat with him on any subject except school. All too soon, they were turning off the highway towards the site. Less than a mile from their destination, they saw a coffee shop and decided to pull in to discuss the plan.

"Principal Banks, what do you want me to do while you go inside? Do I wait in the car?"

"First, for this trip only, it's Olivia. If I ever hear that name in school, I'll respond with, 'Yes, you may have a detention.' Second, I don't want you with me, even in the Explorer. I think the wisest plan is for you to wait here in the coffee shop until I'm done. Then you go do your thing."

"Okay, *Olivia*, I agree you should go in alone. But I think you should drop me off just before the entrance. I'll walk in through the conservation land, but I'll still be able to watch you the whole time. If anything happens, I'll call for help. Once it gets dark enough, I'll put my equipment in place and get out of there."

She thought for a moment. "I guess that works. I'm more worried about you than me. Text me when you're going in. I'll give you 45 minutes to set everything up. If you don't come back, I'll make a call to the local police indicating you were hunting and are lost."

"Deal! Here are the two units you need to plug in near the coffee area." He handed her what looked like two small air fresheners.

Slipping them into her purse, she asked, "Do I have to do anything to turn them on?"

Shaking his head, Alex responded, "No, but try to give them a wipe to take your fingerprints off after you plug them in. Also, only get them out when you're by the coffee area. Their cameras don't cover that area, probably by the security team's design."

Assigned Process Sensors

In the SUV, Alex pulled on his coveralls and prepared his equipment in the back seat as she drove the last mile. Olivia stopped momentarily in front of the entrance to the conservation land, and he slipped out. He walked quickly but quietly along the path that ran parallel to the building's driveway.

As he got into position behind a large tree, he saw her collect the materials and exit the SUV. He observed the security guard watching her step out of the vehicle. As she emerged, she shook out her long blond hair she typically wore in a bun. In her heels, she was well over six feet tall, and Alex was confident she had the guard's attention. Sure enough, the man came and opened the door for her to enter.

Olivia gave the guard a big smile as he held the door. "Thank you so much. It's been a long day." She held out her hand. "Olivia. I'm hoping I can see the site manager. I represent a landscaping company that also provides snow removal services."

The man said, "Very nice to meet you, Olivia. I'm Charlie. I'll see if Ms. DeCosta can see you."

Olivia walked over to the coffee area. She took some lipstick from her purse as she pretended to look in a mirror on the wall. When Charlie looked away for a moment, she slipped the first device into an outlet over the counter.

Walking over to the far wall, she leaned over and appeared to be adjusting her left shoe. Seeing Charlie turn his back on her, she plugged the second unit next to the refrigerator. She then got a bottle of water out of the mini-fridge and turned back to Charlie.

Charlie hung up the phone. "My apologies. Ms. DeCosta is busy and doesn't have time to see you. She has asked if you could leave information with me, and she'll let you know if she's interested."

Olivia smiled and said, "I understand. Here's our brochure with the list of services we provide. We are very interested in expanding in this direction. I'm sure we'll be very competitive."

Charlie thanked her and walked her to the door. He watched her closely as she got into the vehicle and left.

Alex looked at his watch. Waiting 30 minutes, he was pleased when almost all of the cars in the lot left promptly at 5:00 pm. At 5:15, he texted Principal Banks one word, 'In,' and slid through the trees to the target area. Finding a tree covering the front entrance, Alex set up the first camera in a location that should provide enough light to power the battery without being too visible. He positioned the second unit further back so it would cover both the front and back doors.

With both cameras in place, Alex walked between the two and quickly turned on his phone. Pulling up the correct website, he was able to toggle between the two images. Satisfied everything was working, he shut down his phone and started to move out.

Charlie was still at his desk thinking about the attractive saleswoman when he saw a light in the trees just beyond the entrance. The boss had said to be on the lookout, so he decided he better investigate. Grabbing a flashlight, he headed for the door.

Alex thought he was in the clear until he saw the security guard get up from his desk and walk in his direction. He knew he could run, and they would never catch him, but they would likely search the area and find the cameras.

Olivia smiled when she first saw one camera, and then the other, become active. Looking at her watch, she estimated it would only take five more minutes for Alex to emerge from the woods. As she prepared to go, she saw the security guard approaching the door in the closest image. Moments later, Alex walked into the scene. He appeared relaxed and was gesturing as he spoke. She bit her lip and hoped he could pull this off.

Alex walked directly toward the security guard by the door. "Excuse me, Sir. I'm so sorry. I was hunting on the conservation land and waited too long before coming out. I think I got turned around." Gesturing toward the conservation land, he said, "I think my trail out of the woods is right over there."

Charlie looked at him suspiciously but asked him, "What type of bow is that? A Bear?"

Alex smiled. "Diamond Archery. My cousin hunts with a vintage Black Bear Hunter that was our uncle's. I'm not good enough to hunt with a recurve just yet."

Charlie nodded. "I used to. Was a good while ago. Okay, if you walk through the gap in the trees right there," he pointed the way, "you'll be on the conservation trail. Be more careful next time."

"Thank you! I guarantee I will."

Once he was almost back to the road, Alex sent the text "Out." Seeing the SUV pull up, he placed the bow in the back and climbed in. Smiling at Principal Banks, he said, "I like this hair-down look. You should come to school like that."

"Yeah, NOT going to happen." They both laughed in relief as they started the long drive home.

Assigned Process Sensors – Detention Area

During the weeks of their captivity, the two professors had fallen into a routine. While the western Massachusetts facility was dreary, they dreaded the finality of moving to the new research lab. Their hope was Ajax could communicate their current location, and somehow someone would rescue them. Once they moved, they knew the likelihood of rescue would decrease significantly.

Initially, they had kept busy designing the new lab. The revised plan dramatically exceeded their facilities at the university, and they had hoped the complexity would slow down the transfer. They were surprised to find it lengthened the schedule only slightly.

Without access to the internet or any form of external communication, they were starting to go stir crazy and even got short with each other. Jens asked for and received access to security camera footage. The highlight during their days was to watch for wildlife and the occasional human visitor.

Silently signaling Indira, Jens hid his interest as he watched Noah's principal, Ms. Banks, come up to the building. Without sound, there was no way of determining the purported reason for the visit, but the actual intent had to be surveillance.

The bigger surprise came a little later when a young man in camouflage with archery equipment stepped out of the woods to talk to the security guard. The image wasn't clear, but his size and the way he moved were consistent with Noah's friend, Alex.

When the guard came with their dinner, Jens asked if they could stop by the lobby that evening. "It's been quite a long time since we were allowed to see the outdoors. We would greatly appreciate being able to enjoy a coffee before bed in the lounge area."

The guard grudgingly indicated he would relay their request.

New Research Center

Seven and Kate toured the new facility. Everything was to specification, slightly below budget, and on time. "This is excellent work, Kate. I'm pleased you were able to get all of the requested changes completed within your revised timeline."

Kate smiled and added, "It was a team effort. Our general contractor was exceptional. I also appreciate your timely responses to our questions and suggestions. And to be frank, your budget allowed us to bring in the very best sub-contractors."

Seven's phone chirped, and he apologized as he stepped away. While Kate couldn't hear the conversation, it was clear it was not good news. When he returned, he said, "Unfortunately, I'm going to have cut the tour short. I need a private room with secure Wi-Fi."

Kate brought him to the room that was slated to be his office. She said, "Technically, we don't have an occupancy permit, but I've been using this space to work in when I'm here. I've set up temporary Wi-Fi. Text me if you need anything. We have coffee and donuts if you'd like them."

"Thank you, Kate."

Seven quickly set up his laptop and connected to the internet. Clicking the secured link, he opened the chatbox.

Chairman: I just received a notice indicating you have an update.

Seven: I do. We have made significant progress, but it appears there is also a setback.

Chairman: What's the progress?

Seven: The research facility is ready. We should be able to move the professors in shortly.

Chairman: This is ahead of schedule. Are the professors cooperating?

Seven: Yes. They believe we will let them go once the project achieves specific milestones.

Chairman: I'm assuming that is not your plan.

Seven: No. It isn't. We plan to capture their children and use them as leverage.

Chairman: And how is it going?

Seven: This brings us to the setback. The boy has eluded us.

Chairman: How can a young boy elude one of our best teams?

Seven: It appears he had local help. We are considering an alternate approach.

Chairman: Which is?

Seven: Convince the boy and girl it's in their best interest to come to us.

Chairman: Get it done and report back. Move the professors soon.

PART 5

Bangor, Maine

Noah and Sasha walked off the plane into the airport, unsure what to do next. Exiting the secure area to baggage claim, Sasha suddenly went into full alert and then did her excited little skip. Noah looked and then said, "Kellen? Where?"

Sasha was already moving through the crowd. Noah could barely keep up, holding the leash they used when in public. She went around a pole and, with a sudden surge of speed, pulled out of Noah's hands. When Noah caught up with her, she had her front paws on Kellen's chest. His head was against hers, and Noah heard him say, "So good to see you...."

After a moment, Kellen looked over to Noah. Sasha dropped down, and Kellen wrapped Noah up in a bear hug. "I'm so glad you guys are safe." Looking at Sasha, he said, "Yeah, I know you were there, but still." With her little look of fake disgust, he rolled his eyes and said, "Fine. You had everything under control the whole time."

Kellen became serious and looked around. "I think we gave them the slip by flying you here. But I'm sure they'll figure it out soon. Let's get going. I borrowed a car I need to return. We'll stay the night at a friend's apartment that's not too far from here."

Kellen's friend was out of town, so they had his apartment to themselves. Ordering in pizza and grilled chicken and rice, they had a chance to catch up over dinner. First, Noah and Sasha wanted to know all about Kellen and his recovery. Next, Noah and Sasha recounted all of their adventures since they had been separated.

Finally, Noah asked about Avi. Kellen explained her situation and said they would join her tomorrow. When he came to the part about the need for a ferry ride, Sasha's ears went back. Kellen said, "What?"

Noah frowned, "Her recent encounters with boats have been, let's say, unpleasant."

Kellen watched her reaction and said, "No. It's going to be no big deal. The captain is an old friend and knows the sea better than anyone I've ever met. No, the boat doesn't go fast. The weather's going to be fine tomorrow."

Sasha huffed off and curled up in a corner. Kellen admitted to Noah, "Ajax doesn't care for boats either. Hates the feeling of movement under his feet." He thought for a moment. "Hey, I have other big news."

Kellen went to his bag and pulled out his laptop. He booted it up and brought up a website. It took Noah a moment before he realized he was watching the Assigned Process Sensors building. Kellen smiled and nodded. "Yup, Alex was successful. Diego has a program that sorts through the hours of nothingness and isolates just the moments when something happens. He'll start posting the summaries tomorrow."

Sasha came over and watched, too. Kellen answered her question, "No audio from these cameras. But check this out." He clicked on a link to another site. Soft noises came from the computer. Then there was the sound of a door opening.

"Yeah, I know it doesn't sound like much, but that's the composite audio from two listening devices in the lobby. We know the guards tend to stop by and chat at the coffee station."

Noah and Sasha were both excited. Noah asked, "Does Diego have a program that organizes the audio data?"

"He does. We're going to start reviewing the first files tomorrow afternoon when we arrive."

Noah rubbed his hands together. The pieces were falling into place. He could hardly wait to get started.

The Coast of Maine

Avi and Ajax ran down to the dock when they heard Ann announce the ferry had entered the harbor. As usual, Hank drew the boat alongside the pier as Tim secured the lines. Noah stepped off first and ran to meet the two of them. Sasha seemed to be in a bit of a quandary as she felt Ajax watching. Finally, she hopped up on the step and over onto the dock. She trotted over and gently pushed her head into Avi, getting a big hug in return. Sasha seemed to try to be nonchalant around Ajax, but everyone could sense the excitement in both of them.

Hank waved goodbye and called out to Ann that he needed to run some mail out to Reed's Point. He'd be an hour later than usual. Ann turned to the group and said, "Well, that's good I suppose, since I think I'll need to take two trips in the skiff to get us all back."

Sasha's eyes went to the little boat. She turned back to Ajax, and those that could understand her knew she was asking if there was any other way.

Ajax turned to Avi and communicated an alternate plan to her. She responded, "I suppose the two of you could take the trail back." She looked to Noah, and he shrugged and nodded. Seeing Sasha communicating to Noah, Avi responded before he had a chance. "It's about five miles, and it certainly should be safe. And yes, we're in good hands."

Kellen glanced at Noah and smiled. "Looks like Avi's got the language down pretty well. It seems she was more diligent than my last student."

Noah laughed and said, "You mean that kid, Noah? He's a big goof off. Of course, he might be more attentive if his partner didn't keep biting him."

Sasha gave him a playful nip, and everyone laughed. Ajax was already turning and trotting off the pier. Sasha gave a quick goodbye and ran after him. The group watched as they ran next to one another up the hill to the trail. Kellen said what they were all thinking, "Wow! What an amazing pair."

Ann turned to Avi, "I know they're very smart, but are you sure they know how to get back?"

"Ajax knows his way around here and won't be late for dinner. If you're worried about their safety, I think anyone or anything foolish enough to mess with them would wish they hadn't." As Avi said it, she wondered if they had other motivations for wanting to be alone.

The Trail

Sasha trotted next to Ajax. The trail wound along the coast and at times came out to look over the ocean. The scents, the sounds, and the scenery were all mesmerizing. At one point, Ajax paused and looked out over a particularly dramatic cliff. The breeze from the ocean ruffled his fur, and the soft light of the late afternoon sun seemed to make his dark coat sparkle.

He turned to her and expressed his happiness. She moved closer and breathed in his scent. She signed how much she liked him but then worried how he would interpret it. Her answer was immediate when he laid his head against her shoulder.

Alex's House

Diego and Nico ran up to Alex's door and banged furiously. Alex's mom came to the door and said, "Guys, what's going on?"

"Mrs. Levine, is Alex here? We need to talk to him right away." Breathless from the run over, Diego could hardly get the words out.

"He just texted he is about five minutes away. Would you like some cookies and milk while you wait? Chocolate chip, right out of the oven."

Nico smiled and said, "Absolutely!" He winked at Diego. Alex's mom made the best cookies. Diego frowned since he was dying to tell Alex what he knew and felt this might result in a delay.

The two boys were at the table chatting with his mom when Alex walked in from soccer practice. "What's going on here?" He saw the look on Diego's face but knew he couldn't just run to his room without raising suspicion from his mom.

As Alex sat down to a cookie, Diego blurted out, "We got some surprising results on our project!"

Alex took a moment to savor what was indeed a fantastic cookie before asking, "Isn't it early to get results?" Seeing Diego about to burst, he turned to his mom. "Can we grab some cookies and go to my room? I think Diego is pretty excited."

Laughing, Mrs. Levine put some cookies on a tray and gave each boy a top off on their milk. "Not too long, Alex, dinner is at 5:00. And don't completely ruin your appetites on those cookies." She shook her head, knowing there was little chance of that given those boys' appetites.

When they got into his room, Alex turned to Diego and said, "What's so urgent?"

"You need to hear this." Diego was setting up his laptop and plugging in some noise-canceling headphones. "A lot of it is soft, so I had Nico run it through his voice-to-text program. If you watch the screen, the text syncs with the audio."

Alex listened to what sounded like rustling for the first 30 seconds. Then he heard a woman's voice speaking softly. The text feature displayed her conversation.

Isn't it awesome to be able to have a real cup of coffee? And to be able to see the outside! We appreciate this.

Alex's eyes got big. Pausing the recording, he said, "That's Avi's mom!"

Diego nodded, "It is. And wait, it gets better."

Alex resumed the recording and could hear a man's voice speaking a bit louder.

This is very nice. We need to thank you, Charlie, for allowing this.

"Noah's dad. This recording confirms they're both at the facility." Diego was grinning ear to ear. "But hold on. There's still more. The big reveal is coming."

After a moment, a third voice could barely be heard. Alex couldn't make out the words, but the transcript made Alex take a deep breath in surprise.

Well, it was Mister Seven who said it was okay. I'm sorry that you're being held here, but I've been told it's a matter of national security. My understanding is it won't be much longer. You'll be transferred in three days, and I'll be out of a job.

After almost a minute of minimal sound and no transcript, Alex stopped the recording. "Is there more?"

Diego made a face, "We, and by we, I mean Nico, couldn't get anything else to transcribe. The last transcript may be wrong."

Nico jumped in finally, "No way. My diagnostics indicate a 97 percent probability for the last section. That's what the guard said."

Alex looked at his friends, "We've got to tell the others!"

The Coast of Maine – Ann and Hank's House

Kellen looked over at the disposable phone that had just dinged, indicating a message had arrived. Only one person had the number. Looking over at Ann, she nodded her approval to leave the dinner table.

Kellen retrieved the phone and reviewed the text history. There was just one message received a minute ago.

A: Big news from the audio. Need to talk.

Kellen quickly typed in a reply.

K: Usual place in 5 minutes

Nodding at the others to go to the office, Kellen apologized to Ann and Hank for ruining dinner. As usual, Ann was her pragmatic self. "It will all reheat when you folks are ready. Meantime, I hope this is good news."

Avi was already setting up her laptop when Kellen arrived. The communication program started, and she announced their arrival.

AVI → Here with the whole group.

ALEX → Here with Diego and Nico.

AVI → Big news?

ALEX → Huge. See file just uploaded. Audio and visual.

Avi opened the new file. The poor quality of the laptop's speakers made the audio pretty hard to understand. But there was no denying the identity of the first two voices. Then the bombshell announcement was made by the guard.

Everyone in the room with Avi seemed to speak at once. Finally, Kellen let out a screeching whistle. The voices went silent as Hank stuck his head in the room.

"Just what in tarnation is going on in here? Sounds like a pack of coyotes got in the house. Are you guys okay?"

Kellen smiled and said, "I guess we're a bit loud. Sorry, but we got big news. It's all fine."

As Hank left, Kellen turned to Noah and said, "What do you think?"

Noah paused for a moment before saying, "Let's thank Alex, Diego, and Nico and let them go for now. Then I want to discuss what to do."

AVI → We are astounded. You guys are amazing! Need some time to process.

ALEX → Let us know when you need us. We'll be around.

After Avi shut down the laptop, Noah summarized what they had learned. "Well, it appears our folks are being held in the facility Ajax escaped from. It also seems they'll be moved to a new location in just a few days."

Avi chimed in, "I think the new facility will be harder to break into even if we have the location right. I think our best chance to set them free is during their transfer."

Kellen said, "Do we notify the DRIA? They certainly have better resources than we do."

Ajax and Sasha both stepped forward and expressed dissent.

Kellen said, "They got Williams out. They've cleaned house."

Noah agreed with the canines. "I think they've been penetrated above the agent level. I don't trust them. Plus, they've made no progress finding our parents, or for that matter, us. I think someone is dissuading them from trying."

Avi nodded, "I think we need to do this ourselves. But we don't have any resources."

Ajax looked at her as he and Sasha stepped forward. Avi balked, "I can't risk losing you guys too!" As Ajax reacted, she wiped away a tear.

Noah hugged her and said, "We've got three choices: Do nothing. Notify the authorities. Figure out how to do it ourselves. I say we go with the last option. We can figure this out. I just need to do more planning."

Hank's voice came from behind them. "I think you have more resources than you counted. Also, as the local law enforcement, I have access to equipment that will reduce our risks. Sorry, couldn't help overhearing, since you guys are louder than a pack of coyotes, as we've already established."

Noah smiled. "Thanks, Hank! Avi, I have this strange feeling that our folks knew we were listening. What do you think?"

"I agree. Let's start monitoring the website we set up. Our parents may try to communicate soon. We will also post a message indicating we heard them."

Assigned Process Sensors – Detention Area

Indira looked over at Jens while sipping her coffee at their communal table. "It's been a day since we had coffee in the lobby. What do you think?"

Realizing their words and actions were being monitored, Jens nodded and responded, "I wish we could see the lobby again, but it's time to focus on getting the laboratory ready. We should start ordering the chemicals necessary for testing the analytical equipment now. It needs to arrive in the next five days if we're going to get the lab set up per Mr. Seven's schedule."

Indira nodded. When they were first becoming concerned that one or more of them might be held and forced to do research, they had some of Noah's friends set up a website. It appeared to be a company that provided ultrapure chemicals exceeding the highest grades reasonable. The site used product availability to convey coded messages. If Noah and Avi had heard their conversation in the lobby, they would likely use this as a method to establish communication.

Indira pushed the button summoning their "Technician," Trent. Neither of the professors liked him, but he was their only means to access the Web. When he finally came, he looked at the two of them through narrowed eyes.

"Whatda ya want?"

"Trent, we'd like to purchase additional chemicals necessary to start the analytical equipment." Indira always spoke to him in a professional tone despite his sullen attitude. "We require ultra-pure lithium hydroxide. It needs to be 99.9999% pure. There's only one company we know of that provides it."

"Whatda ya need it for? We already ordered a bunch of chemicals."

Indira remained even-toned and patient. "We need it to calibrate the Mass Spectrometer." She knew Trent didn't know a Mass Spectrometer from a Mr. Coffee, but someone who reviewed the audio might. She was pretty confident no one here knew how to calibrate one.

After he opened his laptop, she continued in the same slow, even tone. "Trent, please navigate to www.ultrapurechemicals.org." The website Diego and Nico had set up appeared on the screen. "As you can see, you need to enter your customer account. Would you like me to sign in?"

Trent frowned. "No. Mr. Seven was clear. Only I can touch the computer."

Indira smiled. Most people would have warmed with this gesture. Trent was unaffected. She gave him her login credentials and was pleased when the website opened, as she had seen in the demonstration.

"In the Search box, type LiOH."

As Trent followed her instructions, a page came up with the product, but a message appeared.

We are currently out of stock of this product. We have ordered raw materials from our supplier, which are now in transit. We expect to be able to supply this soon.

Indira and Jens shared a look. Out of stock was code that the others knew they were in trouble. They weren't sure what the rest meant.

Indira asked Trent to do one more thing. In the Customer Comments section on this page, she had him type a short message.

We require this product within three days. Please confirm you will be able to ship it to the following address: Luxura Transit Center, 555 County Road 37, Hiram, OH, 44234

Both professors suspected the location where they had shipped all of the other equipment would be near the new research center.

A response appeared after only a moment.

This request is short notice, but we will do our best to accommodate your request. Thank you for using UltraPureChemicals.

Alex's House

Nico was reviewing the latest audio file when a message flashed that a chatbox had been opened on UltraPureChemicals. His excitement made it tough to type the response. He called Alex over, who watched and said, "What do you know? We have contact with the professors."

As he watched Nico type the message, Alex sent Kellen a text to notify Noah and the team.

A: Response to our out-of-stock situation.

Kellen's reply came back immediately:

K: Usual place. 5 Min.

Alex opened the communication program:

ALEX → Here with Nico.

AVI → We are all here.

ALEX → The Profs responded to our out-of-stock message. They need the product in just three days.

The response took several minutes to come back. Alex and Nico knew the group was discussing the next steps. Alex remembered another detail he had forgotten to mention.

ALEX → We heard additional water cooler talk. The guards reaffirmed their guests would be leaving for their new home in two days.

After a moment, the response came back.

AVI → We need you to monitor the video tomorrow in case their plans change. The following day, we need tracking.

ALEX → We'll be ready.

AVI → Keep us posted.

Alex smiled at Nico. "Looks like we're a go. I'm going to check on Diego's progress in creating the GPS tracker. I'm also hoping Principal Banks is up for another trip to Assigned Process Sensors."

The Coast of Maine – Ann and Hank's House

Noah thought through his resources and the current plan to rescue his dad and Avi's mom. Their assumption was the rescue had the highest likelihood of success during their transfer to the new research facility in Ohio. Even so, there would be a driver and probably one or more guards during the transfer process. He checked over the steps in his plan:

- Develop tracking device (Diego)

- Plant device on the transfer vehicle (Alex)

- Surveillance on the vehicle during loading (Alex with Principal Banks)

- Track vehicle while it's moving (Noah, Avi, Hank, Sasha, Ajax)

- Meet with DRIA, obtain assistance (Kellen)

- Stop vehicle in appropriate location (Officer Jefferson, Hank's friend)

- Disable guards/driver (Hank, Officer Jefferson, DRIA?)

- Get professors out of vehicle (TBD)

Noah knew this was a relatively complex plan, and it required assistance from Hank and his friend, but he saw no other way. He also had no idea how they would get their parents out if they were somehow locked up. The driver might cooperate, but he hoped Hank would come up with an alternate solution.

Hank came over and looked at the list. He broke into a small smile when he saw the last bullet. "I do believe we have that covered."

Alex's House

Alex looked over the tracking device handed to him. As usual, Diego had outdone himself. The device was just slightly larger than a cell phone and about twice as thick. It was contained inside a small gray metal box and looked utterly nondescript. Looking over at Diego, he said, "Alright, let's go through this again."

Diego smiled and patiently explained, "The first step is to activate the device by sliding it open." He paused and showed him how the box slid open. "Then turn on the power. Your phone will receive a text message and vibrate, so no lights, no need to take it out. Then close the case and attach it."

"Couldn't we have attached it with a magnet or something simple?" Alex looked at the zip ties he would use to attach the device. He could just imagine trying to get them into place in the dark.

"Sorry, Alex, I tried magnetic mounting, but it kept interfering with the electronics, even with shielding. I think there will be someplace under the vehicle that will work, but without seeing it, I can't tell you what it will be."

Alex raised his eyebrows, "Okay, we'll make it work. And the battery should last at least two days?"

Diego nodded. "This is a modification of an off-the-shelf unit that normally is powered by the vehicle's electrical system. I made it self-contained. Also notice that it reports out via a cellular signal. No cell coverage means it will temporarily drop out, but I think it shouldn't be too much of a problem."

Alex clapped him on the shoulder as Nico walked in with a plate full of cookies. Speaking around one, he said, "Alex, nothing to worry about. Also, Diego and I will monitor everything on the cameras and audio from here. We'll let you know if anything goes astray."

Diego looked at the clock. "Shouldn't Principal Banks be here soon?" As Alex nodded, Diego winked at Nico and added, "I hear you told Nico she's really pretty with her hair down." The two younger boys grinned.

Alex frowned, "Guys, stop it. She's pulling in now. I got to go, and I need to focus." He grabbed the equipment, and the three of them walked to the front porch. Once there, they put their three fists together in a triangle and simultaneously said, "LUCK!"

On the Road, Somewhere in Maine

Hank's Rose Point jurisdiction had only one emergency vehicle, a four-wheel-drive pickup with a crew cab. Driving the rough dirt roads out to the main road took over an hour. When Kellen commented, Hank said dryly, "There's a reason people come in on the ferry."

Once on the highway, Hank drove the truck with such care the trek down to western Massachusetts seemed to take forever. Fortunately, the plan was to get close to the area a day early and connect with Officer Jefferson.

Noah reviewed the steps for about the hundredth time, causing Avi to groan. "Noah, stop reviewing. Let's check the cameras and audio."

Before Noah could get the app for the cameras pulled up on his phone, a text came in from Diego.

D: Check the video feed. Large van pulling into the site.

D: It has a creepy feeling about it.

Noah pulled up his video feed. He responded:

N: We see it now. I think this is it. Audio?

D: We hear chatter. Mentioning, "Guests leaving tonight."

Noah glanced at Kellen and raised his eyebrows. Kellen responded, "On it," and pulled out his phone to move up his meeting with the DRIA.

Noah turned to Hank, "Can we get there by this evening? I think everything just got accelerated." Noah saw the speedometer creep up above the speed limit.

"No problem for us. We better reach out to Tom." Hank handed his phone to Avi to initiate the call.

"Wait. Tom Jefferson? You're kidding, right?" Avi noticed even Ajax and Sasha seemed to understand the reference.

"Yeah, his folks had a sense of humor. Everyone hold on. We're going to need to push it to get there."

On the Road, Western Massachusetts

Alex glanced over at Principal Banks and relayed the message. "Diego just texted that the van is there. They might be moving tonight." Looking down at her camouflage pants, he continued, "I think it's better if I go in alone."

"Nonsense. I'm going in with you. It's still archery season. We can go in fully camouflaged."

They pulled off the highway at the same café they had stopped at previously. After a quick snack, a review of the plans, and one last protest from Alex, they drove the last couple of miles.

Conservation Land

The conservation land had a small parking area not visible from the road. With the vehicle hidden, they put on their camo jackets. Carrying the two bows, they slowly made their way down the overgrown path. Alex noticed Olivia moved silently through the woods. She was careful not to step on sticks or let branches brush against her. When she saw him watching, she leaned over and whispered in his ear, "I grew up in the country."

They reached the place Alex had selected as the observation point. They had a good view of the truck and would be able to see anyone who entered it. The original plan was to wait until it was darker before attaching the tracker. They would then use night vision goggles to monitor the truck. The approach changed when Diego sent a text.

D: Chatter says moving the prisoners NOW!

Alex quickly responded.

A: Attempting to attach the tracker.

Alex crept silently through the woods while Olivia watched the doors. He carefully skirted areas covered by the building's security cameras. In the final approach, the van shielded him from the closest camera. There was only a distance of about ten yards where he would be visible, but some low pines provided a little cover.

Reaching the van, he slid underneath and quickly found a suitable location for the tracker. Turning it on, he felt his phone vibrate in his pocket, indicating it was active. The zip ties worked perfectly, and he was done in under a minute.

Just as he stood back up, he heard the door to the facility open. He flattened against the side of the van next to the rear wheel. Two guards emerged talking about plans for the weekend. Holding his breath, he waited until the guards were inside the cab of the vehicle before making his way into the low brush.

"Hey, did you just hear something?" Alex dropped down into the scrub as the two men exited the vehicle and looked his way.

Principal Banks had been watching Alex, and she knew she needed to do something when the guards looked in his direction. Picking up a fist-sized rock, she tossed it into the woods away from Alex. It must have hit something soft, because it didn't make any audible sound. She tried throwing a second rock and was rewarded when two doves were startled and flew out. The guards saw them, nodded at each other, and went back into the van.

Alex returned to their observation point and whispered, "Doves?"

The principal smiled and whispered back, "Right on cue."

Assigned Process Sensors

Jens and Indira were watching the security feed when they saw the ominous black van pull into the facility. After the driver parked by the back door, they scrutinized the vehicle intently to learn any clues about their upcoming trip. They were studying the monitor when Charlie stopped by.

"Well, it appears you will be leaving shortly. Might want to pack up anything you want to take. I know you don't have much, but there are a couple of totes outside for you to use."

As Charlie was speaking, Jens noticed someone sneaking out of the woods towards the van. As the guard started to turn toward the monitor, Jens spilled his coffee on Charlie's arm.

"I am so sorry." Jens signaled to Indira as she came over with a towel.

"Charlie, here, let me clean that. Jens, you're so clumsy. Charlie, are you hurt?"

The guard was so distracted by the pretty woman cleaning his arm that he never looked back at the screen. After a moment, he remembered his original task.

"Almost forgot. You're heading out in 45 minutes. I'm sorry to see you go. I'm glad we could provide a safe place for you."

The two scientists just nodded. Seven had warned them on the ramifications of trying to alert the guards to their actual situation.

After the 45 minutes had passed, two men came to get them. They told Jens and Indira not to worry about the totes with their things. Someone would pick them up later. The men escorted the two of them down the hallway and out of the building.

When the back doors to the van opened, the professors could see their accommodations for the trip. Two seats that reclined were bolted into the floor. Seat belts were provided for safety, but there were no additional restraints. A cooler was in the corner by what appeared to be a small closet. A tote with some blankets was placed behind the seats.

After exchanging a glance with Jens, Indira pointed at the closet. "The commode?" When one of the men nodded, she said, "So once we get in, we don't get out until we reach our destination?" He nodded again.

Jens looked at the padlock that would keep them locked in. "What if we have an emergency?"

The guard shrugged. "We'll be monitoring you. You'll be fine. Now let's go. We've got a lot of driving to do."

On the Road, Southwestern Vermont

Noah heard the text arrive on the disposable phone. It was Alex with an update from the site:

A: The tracker is in place. Parents entering the van now.

N: Number of guards?

A: Looks like a driver and 1 guard.

N: Is anyone in the back with them?

A: No. But the door has a large padlock.

N: We have a plan for dealing with the lock.

Noah looked over at Hank. "Will we catch up with the van?"

Hank thought for a moment and did some mental calculations. "They'll catch up with us. I'm banking on them taking the highway across. They could fool us and take back roads, but that's what the tracker is for."

Noah opened the application on his phone. The truck hadn't moved yet, so they couldn't confirm the GPS tracker was working. He looked at the map and pointed to where Tom was planning to intercept the vehicle. Avi and Hank nodded.

A: Van is moving.

N: Tracker signal is working.

Avi looked over and saw Sasha and Ajax curled up on the back seat listening intently. Her confidence was rising. They had the resources, and everything seemed to be falling into place.

In the Back of the Van

The professors each grabbed a bottle of water from the cooler before they left. They confirmed the cooler had drinks, a few sandwiches, and other light snacks. As expected, the guards allowed them to roam free in the back but had suggested they keep their seatbelts on if they weren't up and moving around.

After only a short time, it was evident the van had merged onto the highway. There was no heat in the back, but blankets kept them comfortable. Jens glanced up at the camera monitoring them, and Indira nodded. Sitting in the seat closest to the front of the van, Jens laid his head against the wall between the front cab and the back. As he pretended to sleep, he listened intently. He could faintly hear the conversation between the two men in the cab.

On the Road, Western Massachusetts

Noah tracked the direction of the van, which so far, was moving as expected. "It appears they are dropping down to take the Pike."

Hank glanced at Noah's phone and then the GPS. "They're about 45 minutes behind us. I estimate they'll pass Tom in just over an hour. I think we should pull over and get ready. There's a rest stop about seven miles ahead."

As Noah watched, the signal for the van suddenly disappeared. "Signal just went black."

Avi peered over Noah's shoulder. "Did they stop moving before the signal was lost? I think they're passing through a zone with no cell coverage. There aren't too many other routes they can take. Most of the back roads are pretty slow."

As they approached the rest stop, Noah and Avi watched intently and breathed a sigh of relief when the signal reappeared. Everyone in the vehicle seemed tense except Hank. Avi looked over at Noah and raised her eyebrows. Looking back at Hank, she asked the question on both their minds.

"Hank, you don't seem to be too worried about all of this. Have you done stuff like this before? I mean, you were in the Coast Guard, right?"

"Tom and I, well, we go way back. It's true we served in the Coast Guard, but we were part of the Deployable Operations Group. We've done some things."

As they pulled into the rest area, Noah turned his phone so that Avi could see the screen. It showed a web page explaining the D.O.G. was established to put several Special Forces groups under one command within the Coast Guard Special Operations. Hank caught sight of the screen and nodded, "That's the one. It disbanded in 2013. I don't try to keep up with the current organization."

Hank moved around the back of the truck and opened a bin. He pulled out what looked like a vest and nodded to Ajax. Hank placed the ballistic armor on Ajax's back and made some adjustments. "I borrowed these from a friend who works in a K-9 unit. It doesn't cover everything, but it helps."

He then turned to Sasha. As he put her armor on, Hank said, "This will also help you blend in a bit more. Your white coat is pretty, but this will make you a lot less visible."

Hank handed Noah and Avi vests that would fit them, but he cautioned, "I'm having you put these on for added safety. That doesn't mean I want to see you anywhere outside the truck when I stop. Understood?"

Both of them nodded. They watched as Hank fastened a pistol to his belt and took a rifle with a scope out of the gun rack. He carefully placed it on the front seat of the pickup.

"So, here's what's going to happen. After we get back on the road, the van will pass us in ten minutes. We'll stay back about 200 yards until we see Tom pull onto the road and initiate the traffic stop. Tom will pull in behind the van such that the front of his car angles out onto the highway. That'll provide him cover while he orders the driver to get out."

Hank continued, "I'll pull in behind Tom and face the other direction. I'll move into position to cover the passenger's side, but the risk is the guard may get out before I'm ready." Gesturing at Ajax and Sasha, he added, "If that happens, I want you two to slip out and track the guard if he gets into the woods."

Hank then looked to Avi and Noah, "Do they understand?" When they both nodded, he turned back to the canines. "No engaging! Just track him. Noah, I need you to open the door for the dogs and throw the flares onto the highway, so no one gets hit by a car."

Handing Avi his cell phone, he opened an app. "This will track the dogs' vests. I'll need you to locate the guard if he runs into the woods."

The last thing Hank did was grab some light blankets from the bed of the truck. Glancing at his watch, he said, "Time for us to leave. I know it will be a tight squeeze, but I want you all to be in the back seat and cover up with these blankets, so they don't see you."

Inside the Van on the Turnpike

The driver glanced over at the guard riding shotgun. "How're they doing back there?"

The man looked at his video screen. "Sleeping like babies. Do you think anyone's going to come for them?"

"I doubt it. But Seven was adamant. He thinks they'll make an attempt."

The guard patted the case for an AR-15 assault rifle. "We'll be ready if they do. Plus, help is nearby."

The miles clicked by, and the guard said, "Hey, look at that. Strange to see a police truck from Maine way out here." The driver just grunted as they passed it, going slightly above the speed limit.

About a minute later, the driver looked in his rearview mirror and said, "What's this about?"

The guard straightened up. Police lights were flashing in the side mirror. Switching his feed to a camera on the rear door, he announced, "One local boy. Not a trooper. Why is he pulling us over here on the Pike?"

The driver pulled into the break-down lane and noticed the patrolman was not directly behind him; instead, he was parked at an angle. Then he saw the police truck pulling in behind the patrolman, and his lights were flashing as well. "We've got a problem!"

The guard immediately jumped out, rifle in hand, and sprinted for the woods. Once he found cover, he sent a quick text to his colleague in the follower SUV. He cussed when he saw the response, "10 minutes." He set his sights on the patrolman's car and decided to wait before causing a scene. Hopefully, the driver could talk his way out of this.

The Side of the Road

After Hank saw the van pass by, he calmly said, "There they go." About a minute later, he saw the lights from Tom's car as it came out from the hiding spot on the side of the road. As Hank saw Tom take the angled position, he called out, "Hang on!" and turned on the emergency lights. He pulled in and positioned the truck to face the woods. Sliding across the bench seat, he exited on the passenger side.

As Hank grabbed his rifle, he saw the guard running into the woods. Hank signaled to Noah to open the door and let Ajax and Sasha out.

Tom, focused on the driver's side of the van, called out, "DRIVER OF THE VAN! EXIT NOW WITH YOUR HANDS IN THE AIR! TELL YOUR PASSENGER TO COME OUT OF THE WOODS!" Tom glanced back to look at the pickup. Hank was positioned behind the passenger front tire, with his rifle aimed at the woods.

Sasha and Ajax entered the woods. They could hear and smell the man ahead of them as he found cover. After moving silently to his ten and two o'clock positions, they each crept forward about six feet.

Avi called out to Hank. "They found him parallel to the passenger door of the van, 15 feet into the woods."

Hank scanned the area with his thermal scope. He found the man positioned behind a rock, aiming his rifle at Tom. Hank fired a shot that hit the rock near the man's head. As the shooter attempted to move, Hank fired a second shot meant to hold him in position. Instead, the man attempted to run towards some large trees for more cover. Unexpectedly, his foot caught on a root, and he pitched forward hitting his head on a rock.

Ajax saw the shooter fall and could smell the blood from his wound. He carefully edged forward to assess the situation. The man lay motionless but was breathing. He was badly hurt and would require medical attention. As Sasha moved in, Ajax carefully pulled the rifle away and hid it.

When Hank fired the second shot, Tom looked back with expectation. Hank waited a couple of moments, held up his index finger, and then lowered it. Tom nodded and then called out to the driver again, "DRIVER, EXIT NOW!"

The driver heard a shot, but it wasn't clear what had happened. As he watched the patrolman in the rearview mirror, he looked down at the text chain. The follower SUV would arrive in six minutes. He just needed to find a way to buy time. As he yelled back, "HOW DO I KNOW," the passenger door flew open, and he was staring into the barrel of Hank's pistol. He quickly raised his hands.

Hank tossed the driver a zip tie and ordered, "Fasten your hands to the steering wheel." After ensuring they were secure, Hank took the man's phone and walked back to the group.

"Guys, you need to hear this." Hank held the driver's phone up. "The shooter got a text off. Looks like company is coming in five minutes."

He looked over at Noah. "Are the dogs back?"

"They are both here and are fine." Noah was hugging Sasha while Ajax leaned against her. Noah then asked, "What about the driver?"

Hank replied, "He's zip-tied to the steering wheel. What's the status of the guard?"

"Ajax says he has a serious head wound."

Avi was pacing back and forth at the back of the van. "How are we going to get them out?"

Tom was rummaging around in the trunk of his patrol car. He pulled something out that looked like a robot's hand. "It's called a Strong Arm. Made by the Jaws of Life folks. It's on loan from friends on the SWAT team." Walking over to the back of the van, it took him seconds to get the lock off and the door open. As the professors stepped out, Avi and Noah ran up and embraced them.

"There is no time for this. We overheard the driver and guard. The vehicle following us cannot be far behind." Jens had given Noah a quick hug and then looked over at the two men with them.

Noah said, "They'll be here in a couple of minutes. This is Hank and Tom. They're with us. Kellen is hopefully on his way with additional help. I'll text him now, but he won't be here for a bit."

Service Plaza, Massachusetts Turnpike

Kellen watched as Director Johnston walked through the door. He stood and shook the DRIA Director's hand and said, "Thanks for coming."

"Thanks for coming? General Clayton was right. You guys staged this whole thing. First, you disappear from the hospital. Now you text me, 'We're going to get the Professors back.' This is a load of bull. I should be arresting you."

Kellen sat silent; teeth clenched. When the Director finished, he said evenly, "Are you done? Got that out of your system? Because the clock's ticking for me. In a few minutes,

I'll either get a text, and we'll have the professors back. Or something will have gone wrong, and people will be hurt. Either way, I could use your help. But I'll go on without it, if necessary."

"You're telling me you and your spy kids figured out where they're keeping the professors?"

"I'm telling you that your house is still dirty. Whoever influenced the General and got you to back off is involved in this. I'm telling you we don't just know where the professors are." He paused as his phone chimed. "We've got them."

The Director looked at the text as Kellen got out of the booth.

N: Got them. More bad guys on the way. Need help ASAP.

The Director looked chagrinned, "I've got myself and three others in the Suburban. They're my best, and I trust them completely."

The two men ran outside and climbed into the vehicle. As the Director pulled out of the service plaza, Kellen texted Noah back.

K: Help is on the way.

The Side of the Road

As Noah looked down to see Kellen's response, he heard Hank say, "SUV coming. It's them. It looks like they're early."

Avi said, "It's too late to get to the cars."

Noah looked at Sasha and nodded. "Sasha says there are some big rocks just inside the woods that will provide cover." The group moved into the woods just as the SUV was pulling in behind the pickup. Noah shot off a quick text to Kellen.

Hank told them, "Take cover behind the rocks. We're going to slow them down." He and Tom positioned themselves behind a couple of three-foot-high boulders closest to the road. "Careful, Tom. Let's not hurt anyone just yet."

As one of the SUV's doors started to open, Tom fired a shot into the passenger-side mirror. Shocked, the men inside ducked down. Hank's rifle fired four more times in quick succession, with him working the bolt action between each shot. Both front tires and the two headlights were shot out.

Seeing the front of the SUV drop, Noah said, "I thought that only worked in movies."

Hank let out a rare chuckle. "Tom's pistol might not make it through the tread. This 30-06 rifle packs a pretty big punch. I figure it should make them think twice."

"That was very nice shooting," Jens said, appreciating the precision.

"With the scope, it isn't much at this distance. Now let's quiet down as I believe they'll attempt to get out of their vehicle." The group watched as Hank moved away from the rock and lay prone on the ground.

Almost another minute went by when they noticed the driver's door of the SUV slowly open. No one appeared, but Hank's rifle boomed again. They heard a shout and then a bunch of cursing. The door quickly shut.

Tom said, "Hank, did you just shoot his foot?"

"It was like threading a needle. I doubt if I got it, but it'll make him think twice about sticking it out there."

Indira spoke up, "What will they do now?"

"Well, they don't seem to be trained professionals or even halfway smart, but my guess is they'll try to back up so they can get out. I counted four heads, and they may have dogs in the back," Hank replied.

In the SUV, the driver stared at his left shoe. His voice cracked as he yelled, "I thought they said it was just going to be a couple of locals and kids out here. Somebody just shot my foot!"

The man in the passenger seat looked over and said, "He just nicked your toe. Now quit whining and back us up!"

Staying low, the driver put the SUV in reverse. He was able to move the disabled vehicle using the backup camera. After only going ten yards, he stopped. "Oh sh*#!"

Inside the Suburban

As they sped down the turnpike, Kellen monitored the tracker that had been placed on the van. He announced they were two miles away when a text arrived from Noah.

N: In the woods, bad guys arrived.

Kellen informed Director Johnston of the text's content. Johnston nodded. As they got closer, they heard several rifle shots. "Everyone, get ready. Kellen, let them know we're arriving."

K: Almost there.

As the Suburban came over a rise, they could see flares and the flashing lights from the patrol car and Hank's truck. Then they saw the backup lights of the SUV as it started to move in reverse.

The Side of the Road

The SUV stopped when the driver saw a Suburban pull off at an angle at the side of the road. Lights on the government vehicle lit up the area as the doors on the passenger side quickly opened. Like shadows, several individuals moved into the darkness. One ran across the road, dropping additional emergency flares along the way.

Recognizing they were out of options, the men in the disabled SUV reluctantly opened their doors and emerged with their hands up. One by one, they were told to walk forward where they were handcuffed and seated by the vehicle. Once they were all there, two agents emerged from the shadows to watch over them. A third agent walked back to talk to a State Trooper who was just pulling up to the scene.

Hank and Tom walked over to the government vehicle. Noah, Avi, and the professors followed ten yards behind, flanked protectively by Sasha and Ajax. Looking at Director Johnston, Hank broke the ice. "Well, Special Agent in Charge Johnston. How very nice of you to stop by."

"It's Director Johnston now, Hank. If I had known you and Tom were here, I'd have had another cup of coffee since I'm sure everything was under control. I'd heard you dropped off the planet."

"Well, *Director*, I'm doing fine acclimating to life as a civilian. You should also know the driver of the van is handcuffed to the steering wheel. His passenger is in the woods and didn't fare as well. He needs attention immediately."

"Understood." The Director then turned towards the professors and said, "I'm glad to see the two of you."

"Are you really? Because it didn't seem like you tried very hard to find us." Indira glared.

"I agree with her, but now is not the time to discuss it. We need to go somewhere private." Jens looked at Noah and Avi. "We know the locations of the sites where we were held and the new laboratory. The Faction will try to cleanse them quickly. We need to get there first."

New Research Center

Seven looked at the message provided from his resource within the Massachusetts State Police. There had been an incident involving the van. Shots had been fired, and someone had been wounded. The casualty was described as a white male, which probably meant one of his men. There was no mention of other passengers, but it was pretty easy to guess the implications, especially since none of his men had made contact with him at the prescribed time for an update.

Someone had intercepted the van. They would have had to deal with six armed men, which meant a government agency, probably the DRIA, was involved. He might be able to use this with the Chairman, but Seven felt it was time to find a quiet place to rethink his career choices.

Looking at his watch, he realized it was time. Opening the chatbox on his computer, the Chairman was already waiting for him.

Chairman: You're late for the update.

Seven: Actually, I am exactly on time. Unfortunately, my punctuality seems to be the only thing that went according to plan this evening.

Chairman: My sources indicate your van was intercepted.

Seven: Yes. It seems likely a government agency, probably the DRIA, was involved.

Chairman: Impossible! I had my colleagues lock them down.

Seven: We'll see about that.

Chairman: We'll see about many things. Your organization's bungling has ruined this operation.

Seven: While I'd love to stay and chat about who is to blame, I suspect they'll get this location out of the driver any minute.

Chairman: Make sure the sites are clean!

Seven: Thank you for your words of wisdom. I will be in touch when it is safe to do so.

As Seven closed his computer and finished packing up, he thought about the Chairman and the Board. Both sites were already clean, and anyone who knew what was going on had been evacuated. But he had left one little package that might have some significant implications. The wildcard was Ajax and his friends. Seven was pretty sure they would be smart enough to figure out the puzzle.

An alarm sounded on his desk. Glancing at the monitor on the wall, he could see there were already two black Suburbans at the outer gate. The alarm changed tone, indicating they had just broken through the lock.

Walking down the hall, he calmly turned into a stairwell leading to the unfinished lower level. Using a small flashlight, Seven proceeded down a long corridor to an exit that required a passcode. Once through, he smiled when he saw the Zero FX electric motorcycle waiting in the dark room. He used his cell phone to check the cameras just outside the door. Confirming it was clear, he pulled on his helmet and opened a pair of wooden doors. From the outside, the building looked like an old shed on the neighboring farm. He could see the lights and hear the voices at the R&D Center. Seven and the bike slipped off into the night with hardly a sound.

Assigned Process Sensors

The group walked through the facility where the professors had been held. Securing the site had taken little effort since the employee roster had been reduced to three guards on a rotating shift. Members of the DRIA reviewed HR records and were already rounding up former employees and detaining them at the local police station. Unfortunately, no one seemed to have an understanding of the real purpose of the site.

Avi and Noah showed Director Johnston the location of the external cameras Alex had placed in the woods outside the facility. They also located the listening devices in the coffee area. Looking at the equipment, the Director was impressed. "One of your friends made these? From parts he found on the internet? I have to meet this kid. I think he needs to come work for us this summer."

Noah promised to provide all of the video and audio recordings to the DRIA, but when he showed him the best images of Seven, the Director just shook his head. None of the footage of Seven captured the man's face. He seemed to have disappeared like a ghost.

There were several clear images of the trainer who had worked with Ajax. When a screenshot was sent to the team searching the facility in Ohio, they replied it matched an individual found electrocuted in the laboratory.

One valuable element found during the raid was information on Separatist Northwest. A backup drive with key contacts was hidden behind the desk of Seven's assistant. Director Johnston assured Jens and Indira they had all of the information needed to disrupt the group for good.

As the Professors shook hands with the Director and thanked him for all of his help, Kellen walked into the lobby with Hank, Tom, Sasha, and Ajax. Kellen pointed back towards the training area as he spoke to the two men, "It's fascinating to see how they set up the training area for Ajax. What do the two of you make of it?" Avi, Noah, and the Professors joined the discussion, interested to hear what men with a military and law enforcement background thought of the approach.

Hank looked at Tom with raised eyebrows, "I'd say they borrowed considerably from canine training for police duty. Would you agree?"

Tom nodded as he said, "Some of it's consistent with what I've seen. But the degree of difficulty and complexity is quite high." He looked over at Ajax and Sasha and winked, "You two are welcome to work with me any day of the week."

Jens looked at the men thoughtfully and said, "Would the two of you consider consulting for us on training? Your background would provide intriguing insights."

Hank shook his head, "I appreciate the offer, but I don't like being away from Ann and Rose Point. As it is, I need to start driving back tonight."

The realization Hank was leaving hit Avi like a wave. She bit her lip as her arms wrapped around him. "Thank you so much. I don't know what we would have done without you!"

Hank blushed as he put his arm around her. His voice was a bit choked up as he said, "Well, Ann and I are planning for you to visit next summer as we discussed. We won't take no for an answer." Looking around the group, he added, "That goes for all of you. You're all welcome any time."

As he said the words, Sasha and Ajax came over and leaned against him. He winked at them and leaned down, and whispered something in their ears.

As the rest of the group came over to thank Hank and say their goodbyes, Jens turned to Tom. "Would you like to work with us, Officer Jefferson?"

"I think I might." Tom paused to look at Sasha and Ajax. "Those two are something special. To be able to work with your team would be interesting. I would need to clear it with my Chief."

"That would be excellent. We greatly appreciate all of your help. What you've done for us was tremendous." Jens shook Tom's hand as he said the words. Indira joined them, and without saying a word, hugged Tom.

Hank nodded to Tom, and the two men walked out the front door to their vehicles.

PART 6

DRIA HQ

Director Johnston put the finishing touches on his report describing the professors' recovery and the subsequent raids on the Assigned Process Sensor locations. He had not directly identified Hank and Tom per their request. Other than that omission, the facts and conclusions were pretty straightforward.

The one bothersome thing was the suicide note found with the leader of Separatist Northwest. The leader claimed his organization was responsible for all of the activities associated with Assigned Process Sensors. There was documentation in his office enabling the DRIA's forensic accountants to unravel the complex financial structure that supported the organization. It all seemed too convenient for the Director.

His thoughts were cut off by Cindy tapping on the door. "Sir, General Clayton has asked if you're ready to discuss the Assigned Process Sensors report. Should I tell his aide you need more time?"

"No, I think I'd like to see the General. I'll stop by after I print off the final copy."

As the aide showed him in, the General turned and stood to greet Director Johnston. "Excellent to see you. Please sit."

The Director took the seat indicated and slid the report over to the General. "I may take one more pass at revising this, but this version is pretty close."

"See? I told you it was Separatist Northwest. The professors were never in any danger."

As he said the words, the Director could see through the General's lie. He stayed silent and watched for further clues from his superior.

"So, are you still holding back on revealing who helped the children?" The General was flipping through the report. "I've told you this is information my superiors consider a top priority."

"General, I've put everything in the report I'm willing to divulge."

"This could be your career. Are you sure?"

"General, my career goes way beyond the walls of this building. If you want me to resign from the DRIA, just say the word."

"Ah, Michael. Always so dramatic. But this may not be my decision to make. Let me review this and get back to you."

The Verma's House

Avi and Noah were hanging out doing homework at the kitchen table. Indira was watching CNN on the television in the other room. Noah nodded towards the noise. "How's it going with your mom?"

Avi's voice was so low it was almost a whisper. "She's still pretty freaked out. She won't leave me alone, even with Ajax staying with us. But I think she's getting better."

Noah rolled his eyes as he noticed the two black ears pop up on the dog bed in the corner. He put his hands on his head, signaling Ajax was listening. Avi giggled.

Avi drew a heart on her paper and wrote Ajax + Sasha. Adding an arrow to the drawing, she giggled again. Noah pointed at the two white ears that popped up next to Ajax's.

"Yeah, my dad was wound pretty tight for a few days, but he seems better." Noah was speaking as softly as Avi. He added in a slightly louder voice, "Dad was reviewing the notes on the food the Faction fed Ajax. He thinks we should consider switching from the chicken and rice blend to the kibble they used."

A pair of low growls sounded from the bed as Avi and Noah burst out laughing. They stopped as Ajax suddenly stood up and, on full alert, ran into the room with the television. An interview was being televised about the raid on the Separatist Northwest's compound. The screen was split between a female reporter and a middle-aged male. The caption below the man's picture read Charles Tanner, Head of the National Technology Security Council.

Tanner was speaking. "...this organization recently orchestrated break-ins at laboratories conducting classified research. It appears their motives were not as simple as what was presented in their propaganda literature."

The reporter nodded and responded, "With the apparent suicide of their leader, Stephan Annapoli, do you think this is the last we've heard of them?"

Noah started to speak when Ajax communicated, "Silence."

After a pause, the man replied, "Tiffany, I am completely confident of that. We take the security of our nation's research programs very seriously. These were bad people. We've taken them down!"

"Thank you for your time, Dr. Tanner. For CNN, this is Tiffany Chen. Back to you, Ted."

Avi asked her mom to mute the volume. "Ajax, what's going on?" His response was so animated Noah had difficulty interpreting it. Avi's jaw dropped, and then she asked, "Are you sure?" She shook her head and quickly said, "Forget I asked that."

Avi turned to Noah, "When he was being held, Ajax overheard that man speak to Seven. Seven called him 'the Chairman.' He's a member of the Faction!"

The Center

The group gathered in the Research Center's conference room. After Avi and Noah explained what Ajax had told them, Jens looked at Indira, who was also looking incredulous. "Ajax, are you saying with absolute certainty Charles Tanner..." He paused.

Indira continued for him, "The Charles Tanner who reviewed all of our proposals is a member of the Faction?"

Ajax's look needed no translation. Avi chimed in, "Ajax is 100% certain. He's also sure Charles Tanner is part of the Faction leadership."

Jens looked at Ajax. "And you heard them communicating?"

Avi added, "Yes. There was a specific number Seven called. A secretary answered, and he recited a code. She then connected him to the Chairman." Avi paused and watched Ajax intently. When he finished, she translated, "Alpha. One. Gold." Avi raised her eyebrows, and Ajax confirmed she had said the code correctly.

"Do we have any way of knowing the number to call?" Indira was looking at Ajax and didn't need a translation to see he didn't know.

Kellen cleared his throat. "Ajax, remember the weird set of commands that were in the training manual? The ones you had never seen before? Do you remember saying it was almost like you were being made to spell out a set of numbers?"

Noah and Avi caught on immediately. Noah looked at Avi, "Do you think?"

"Oh, I'm betting!" She was smiling from ear to ear.

"We suspect Seven feared the transfer might fail. He knew the Faction would blame him and would likely come after him. So, he sent us a message." Noah winked at Avi.

Indira said, "That seems pretty far-fetched. What's the likelihood we would figure this out?"

"It seems pretty 'Sevenish' to me." Looking at Ajax, Avi asked, "Do you think Seven believed you could understand him at the end?" Seeing Ajax's confirmation, she asked further, "How carefully coded were the commands?"

Kellen provided the answer, "It wasn't hard to see they weren't like the rest of the manual. But you would've had to have been familiar with the training to know it."

Jens looked thoughtful. "So, we probably have a telephone number and a code. Don't you think they would have voice recognition in addition to the code?"

Noah watched as Sasha jumped up. "She remembers Seven said each of those words in his last communication to us. Wow, he WAS thinking ahead."

Avi looked at Noah, "We have a number to call, and we can produce an audio recording of Seven saying the code. What's our plan?"

DRIA HQ

Indira had gotten as far as, "We think we know" when Director Johnston held up a finger. She paused as he said, "Before we get into all this work stuff, can we go grab lunch?"

Once outside the office, he glanced around to make sure the three of them were alone before saying, "I'm not feeling too secure in my office these days." As they walked, he listened to the two professors.

"Wait! You mean you guys can communicate with Ajax?" As the Professors explained, providing the minimum amount of information, he just shook his head. "Are you sure Avi can do this?" At the glare from Indira, he stammered, "We all know that little girls...I mean young women..."

Jens interjected, "Their communication is limited, but even we could see Ajax was very excited when he heard Mr. Tanner's voice. We feel strongly it is worth investigating."

The Director bit his lip. "I know Ajax is an amazing dog, but do you think he can be sure? I mean, we're talking about the Head of the National Technology Security Council. He has access to everyone: the President, General Clayton...."

Jens spoke in his most assured voice, the one he used when pitching a project proposal. "There is no risk here. A disposable phone will be used in a remote area. If it's incorrect, they'll tell us we have the wrong number."

"Yeah, but we're talking about bugging his office, right? And then we need to determine how the General is involved."

Indira looked into the Director's eyes, "These people have kidnapped my daughter, my colleague, and myself."

"I didn't say I wouldn't do it. It's just. Well, who needs a pension, right? Particularly if I get a nice suite in Leavenworth."

National Technology Security Office

The telephone rang just once before the female assistant picked up and said, "Priority Code." The response was a correct "Alpha One Gold" designation, but her computer screen showed a code-yellow flag. She said, "Hold, please."

Poking her head into his office, the assistant said, "Mr. Tanner, we have an Alpha One Gold call, but voice recognition indicates a yellow flag."

Finally, thought the Chairman. He was beginning to think Seven was never going to call in. He gave a signal instructing the assistant to trace the call. "Please close the door and transfer the call. I don't want to be disturbed for the next 30 minutes."

The Chairman picked up the phone and replied curtly, "Seven, it's about time."

"This isn't Seven."

"Who are you? How'd you get this number?"

"Let's just say I represent an interested party. We know who you are. We'd like to work with you."

"You have no idea who we are."

"Oh, Mr. Tanner, we know you. We know General Clayton, too. We know the Faction."

The Chairman let out a small involuntary gasp as the caller waited for this to sink in.

The voice continued, "We also know you set up the Separatist group to take the fall in your recent disaster."

"So, what do you want?" The certainty had left the Chairman's voice.

"We want you to work with us. We want the Animal Intelligence Technology you haven't been able to acquire. We have the resources to help you obtain it and bring it to a greater outcome."

"If you're so resourceful, why do you need us?"

"You have connections. Get whatever permission you need. Convene your board if necessary. I'll call you in four days."

The line went dead.

DRIA HQ

As the indicator on the General's secure line lit up, his assistant automatically got up and left his office, closing the door behind him. The General waited a moment before picking up the line.

"Clayton."

"General, it's Tanner. I have news."

"Has our friend appeared?"

"Unfortunately, he hasn't. But yesterday, I had a disturbing discussion with someone who I think is working with him." The Faction Chairman described the basics of the call. "What do you think we should do?"

The General paused a full 15 seconds before answering. "Do we know where it came from?"

"We traced it to a small town in southern Vermont. We tracked the phone down. It was in an envelope behind the counter at a diner. A note was with it that said 'Four Days.' We searched video from local security cameras and questioned people. No one saw anyone put it there or any sign of our friend."

The General paused again. "We need the input of the Board. Tomorrow night at 8:00. The usual spot."

The Center

Jens waited until Director Johnston sat down at the conference table before saying, "Tom informed us his call yesterday with Dr. Tanner went according to plan by following the script we had prepared."

The Director looked around the table. "The children, the dogs? Shouldn't we keep this to a smaller group?"

Jens held his eye. "Everyone in this room has been attacked by these individuals. Several have been wounded. We all deserve to hear this."

Indira asked, "Have you been able to confirm the Faction Chairman is indeed Dr. Charles Tanner, Head of the National Technology Security Council?"

Director Johnston passed around handouts. "Some of you will have to share. It's not an easy read, and I need every copy back when we're done. These are the transcripts from the device I was able to place in Tanner's office. It only captured his side of the conversation. And, of course, this is inadmissible during any form of hearing, but I think it's pretty clear. He's the Chairman."

As the group flipped through the first handout, Johnston handed out a second. "This is a transcript of the Chairman's follow-up call with my boss, the head of the DRIA, General Clayton. We have both sides of the conversation since I had devices in both offices."

Noah caught it first. "The Faction's Board is meeting tomorrow night." Director Johnston smiled and put his finger on his nose.

"I'm not sure of the location yet. I also haven't alerted anyone in my agency because we can't risk someone tipping off General Clayton."

"Do you think either General Clayton or Dr. Tanner will disclose the location?"

The Director shook his head. "I've already removed the devices from their offices because they get swept regularly. But we do know the General is flying into Boston tonight and has a hotel reservation at the Colonial Inn in Concord." He added with a smile, "We should also have real-time knowledge of his location since his aide has a GPS tracker in his watch I happen to have access to."

"Can we expect help from any government agencies?" Noah was already working on the plan.

"Well, I have a friend in the Boston FBI office. He's not willing to participate in any kind of takedown until we have evidence of a conspiracy."

Noah replied, "Perfect. We can provide that. Avi, let's reach out to Diego."

Concord's Colonial Inn

Indira and Kellen stood in front of the reservations desk at the historic Colonial Inn while waiting for the manager. After reviewing the facilities around Concord, the group's consensus was the Faction Board would likely have their meeting in one of the conference rooms at the Inn. Diego had prepared discrete cameras and listening devices that could be placed in the various meeting rooms the Faction might use. He had also developed equipment that was mobile in the event the Board meeting took place elsewhere.

When discussing where to place the devices, Indira had suggested they book a meeting room for the same evening at the Inn. The hope was they could determine which rooms might be used by the Faction. Besides, having their own meeting room would provide a convenient location to meet with the FBI representatives.

"My apologies for the wait. I'm Jennifer, the manager in charge of corporate meetings." The woman reached out and shook their hands.

"Professor Indira Verma, pleased to meet you. This is my colleague, Dr. Kellen Jackson. We're interested in booking a meeting room for tomorrow evening. I apologize. We know this is short notice."

Jennifer put on a pair of glasses and pulled a calendar up on her computer. Turning the screen so they could see, she frowned slightly. "I'm afraid the only ones available are the Merchants' and Middlesex rooms upstairs and the Heritage meeting room downstairs. They are all rather large, accommodating 40 or more people. Would any of these do?"

"Let's book the Heritage room for the entire day. Is it possible to see the other, smaller rooms? We would like to consider your facility for future meetings and typically prefer something a bit cozier."

"That's not a problem. All three are currently open for cleaning. Feel free to take a look around."

Indira smiled and said, "Kellen do you have any other questions?"

He nodded and asked, "Will our reservation be confidential? We are working on sensitive research at the university and need a place offsite to meet discretely with our sponsors."

"Of course. We always treat reservations confidentially unless the party requests a sign for the door."

Kellen and Indira inspected the smaller meeting rooms that were already booked for the following evening: the Thoreau, Alcott, and Prescott. The audio and video cameras Diego had created both appeared and operated as table lamps. The units could be activated remotely and wouldn't be identified in a sweep for devices. Kellen swapped existing lights out with them and attempted to position them so the cameras would be effective.

The Center

In the Center's conference room, Noah received Kellen's text indicating the devices were in place. As Diego turned each one on, the application on Noah's smartphone connected to the devices and showed a visual of the rooms. He texted Kellen to go into each room so he and Diego could confirm the cameras and microphones were working.

Diego smiled as he saw Kellen enter the first room. Listening, they could see and hear his conversation with Indira.

"...this room is more suited for our future meetings. It's just the right size and will make our sponsors feel at home."

The two scientists disappeared from the screen. When they reappeared, they were visible on the screen designated "Room 2." Indira's voice could be heard over the speaker, "I agree this room feels a bit small for our needs. Let's book the Thoreau for our next meeting."

Once they confirmed the equipment was working in the third room, Diego shut everything down. Noah turned to him and said, "What if someone discovers or moves the equipment?"

"If they unplug the equipment, it sends a 'powering down' message. We'll know if it moves, but I'm guessing it'll be fine."

Avi walked into the room. "What if they move the meeting? Or they just have it in one of their rooms?"

Diego nodded, "We know the General's room number, and we would have to get close enough to it to place this device." He held up what looked like a thick *Do Not Disturb* card. "I'm hoping we don't need it. It only gives us audio, and it's fair at best. Nico has hacked into their booking system. We're watching for any other suspicious reservations, but nothing so far."

Holding up an odd-looking harness, Diego continued, "This is what we have if they go offsite. It's a modified GoPro dog harness. We've tried it on Ajax."

Avi rolled her eyes, "Let's hope it doesn't come to that."

Concord's Colonial Inn

The following afternoon Diego supervised the group in setting up the equipment in the Heritage room. Everyone was full of nervous energy, and it was good to have something to keep themselves occupied. They confirmed they could easily switch video between the conference rooms and project the image onto a large screen before they powered down all devices.

Finally, just after 6:00 pm, Director Johnston walked in and looked over the conference room. "You guys do things right. My friend from the FBI and two of his colleagues just arrived for their quiet dinner in the restaurant. I tipped their waitress to make sure they get some complimentary appetizers to slow down the meal."

The Director opened his phone application to be able to track the location of the General's aide. After a few minutes, the aide and the General appeared in the lobby. Kellen received a text from Avi, who was in a sitting area near the front desk.

A: Our two friends just arrived.

K: Are they headed to the conference rooms?

A: They look dressed for the outdoors. Think they are leaving.

The Faction meeting would be in a different location. The group scrambled to implement the alternate plan.

Old North Bridge Visitor Center

The Old North Bridge Visitor Center is located in the Minute Man National Park. A friend of the General was in charge of the site, and he was happy to oblige when asked if it could be used for "official business." The location was a convenient drive for the two other board members. But the real reason the General and the Chairman had selected the site was its history of conflict and rebellion against an oppressive government. As usual, the General and his aide were the first to arrive. The aide confirmed the meeting room did not contain any listening devices or cameras as the Chairman's car pulled into the parking lot.

The Chairman asked his driver to stay outside and watch for potential threats. The driver waited in the chill night air as the General's aide joined him. Rolling his eyes at the absurdity of guarding this location made both military men laugh. They heard the other two cars pull in simultaneously. One contained a man of old New England wealth who led a local venture capital group. The other was occupied by a well-known female president of a nearby university.

The two additional drivers joined the other men already waiting outside the building. The General's aide had brought coffee and donuts. The meetings rarely lasted long, but they all felt something was unusual about this one.

Director Johnston and Kellen waited with Sasha behind a stone wall just across the street. The realization the meeting wouldn't take place at the Colonial Inn had been an unwelcome surprise. They were able to follow the General and his aide to this location but still hadn't figured out how to get inside.

While they waited, Ajax emerged from the shadows. Kellen translated for the Director, "Ajax has found a window in the back of the building that has been left open. He can jump up on a little outbuilding and then onto a small roof by the window to get inside the building." Kellen paused and asked Ajax, "Are you sure you can do it?"

Director Johnston looked amazed. He whispered, "It's incredible. He's talking to you." Pulling out the remote device, he added, "I also can't believe this was put together in a day by that kid, Diego."

The Director and Kellen fastened the camera, external microphone, and transmitter onto Ajax. Kellen whispered to Ajax, "According to Diego, you'll need to be within 15 feet of the group to get usable audio." Kellen turned the devices on and said a little prayer.

Concord's Colonial Inn

Noah, Avi, and Diego were attempting to connect to Ajax's camera when Avi saw it go live on her phone. Diego smiled when a moment later it was projecting onto the big screen in the Heritage meeting room. Jens nodded to Indira, who walked upstairs to the dining room.

Discretely moving over to the three agents, she quietly said, "Excuse me, Gentlemen. Director Johnston of the DRIA asked me to bring you downstairs, where a special dessert is being prepared. Don't worry. We'll take care of the check."

The men stood. One held out his hand and smiled. "Special Projects Agent Bloom. Please show us the desserts."

Old North Bridge Visitor Center

Ajax slipped off into the night. Once he was in position, Kellen and Sasha started running down the road and turned into the Visitor Center. Kellen was wearing his evening running gear, including his headlamp. The four drivers waiting outside the building looked at the runners suspiciously, and two of them put their hands on the pistols holstered under their jackets. Kellen ran right up to them and smiled.

"Sorry to interrupt, Gents. We're just getting in a night run. Passing over the bridge. Is there an event at the Visitor Center?"

As Kellen spoke, Ajax jumped onto a picnic table and then up onto the outbuilding. As he landed, his paws made a slight noise, but the drivers were distracted and didn't notice.

Reaching the Visitor Center required leaping only slightly higher, but the gap was more than five feet. A jump of that distance was typically not much of a challenge for Ajax. Kellen watched as the black shadow approached the edge of the roof and timed his next comment as Ajax made his leap.

"Hope you have a nice night. The smell of your coffee makes me want to get home to get something warm in me."

As Ajax landed on the second roof, his back paws slipped, and he had to throw his body forward to regain balance and not fall. It made only a slight noise, but it was enough for the General's driver to look in that direction.

At that moment, two soft sounds, like "phhhffft," split the air and the General's and Chairman's men fell to the ground with darts in their neck. Per their plan, if any of the drivers looked at Ajax, the DRIA Director would take out the two military men with a dart rifle. In this event, Kellen needed to disable one of the other drivers. He flipped the cover off the needle of a syringe he held in his palm. He surprised himself as he managed to drive the needle into the closest man's arm while he covered the man's mouth with his other hand.

Sasha was tasked with disabling the fourth driver. She wheeled and plowed into his solar plexus, knocking him down and driving the wind out of him. Getting up on one knee, he was reaching into his jacket for a gun when a dart hit him in his neck.

Ajax paused for a second as he watched his friends immobilize the drivers. Slipping through the window, he dropped silently into an upstairs hallway. Padding through the dark building, he found the stairs and walked towards the soft voices below.

Concord's Colonial Inn

Avi involuntarily grabbed Noah's arm as the video showed Ajax's near-miss during his jump to the second roof. When the canine looked back towards his friends on the ground, everything went black. It wasn't clear what was happening on the video monitor. She relaxed slightly when the image returned as Ajax carefully entered through the window.

As the FBI agents and Indira entered the Heritage room, the video was mostly dark shadows, and only the very soft sounds of Ajax walking could be heard. Jens held his finger to his lips as the canine agent continued to move forward. After about a minute, voices could be heard from the audio feed. Ajax turned a corner, and now a group of four people could be seen on the large screen. The Faction's Board Members were standing, sipping coffee and murmuring. Hiding in the shadows, Ajax was invisible to them, but he was able to keep the camera stationary and focused on them as their meeting began.

Dr. Tanner held up a hand. "We should get started. This is not a formal meeting of the Board, but something startling has happened, and I thought we should discuss it."

The University President interjected, "Does this have anything to do with our repeated failed attempts to acquire the 'Protectors' technology?"

"Yes, Silvia. As the three of you know, the man known as Seven disappeared recently."

"You mean the Seven who repeatedly failed to acquire the assets we targeted? The man who then allowed them to slip between his fingers when he finally did get them? That Seven?"

"Charles, please." The Chairman glared at the older man. "I know you're frustrated. We're all frustrated. But please hear me out."

"I recently received a secure call that used Seven's code to contact me. The caller knew who I was. He also knew General Clayton's affiliation with our group. He proposed we work with his organization to reinvigorate our attempts to acquire the researchers and the technology."

The General cleared his throat and spoke for the first time. "We're not certain the offer is legitimate. We haven't been able to identify this individual from the recording or find him at the location where the call was made. He claims to be working with Mr. Seven, but we can't verify that."

As the female board member started to interject, the General held up his finger, "Let me finish, Silvia."

While the group on the screen continued to speak, Special Agent Bloom stood. "We've seen enough. You're capturing all of this, right?" As Noah nodded, Agent Bloom continued, "Does anyone have any details on the current situation?"

Jens replied, "I just got a text. Director Johnston is onsite, and the drivers have been immobilized. How should I respond?"

Bloom gave a slight smile, "Tell them help is on the way."

PART 7

On the Beach of a Caribbean Island

Seven sipped his strawberry daiquiri as he scrolled on his iPad through the various articles that described the capture of the Faction. The public was outraged over a conspiracy that reached the highest levels of the government. The head of the National Technology Security Council and a two-star general had attempted to steal technology funded for national defense purposes. He smiled, thinking about the downfall of the smug, ruthless Chairman.

What surprised Seven was the ability of the DRIA to keep the highest-priority technology, the Protectors, out of the narrative. While there was mention of genetically-modified animals, it was just one of many research areas listed. The articles seemed to focus more on weapons and communication technology and the associated risks of them being turned over to the country's enemies.

Likewise, the articles never mentioned that the Faction had kidnapped and held the scientists against their will. It seemed the agencies involved didn't want citizens to know researchers with access to sensitive security secrets were potentially at risk.

Regardless, the drinks were cold, and he had enough money set aside for an extended vacation before he got back to work. Not that it was all relaxation. He thought about the thick dossier he had developed on Ajax and the thinner compilation he had on Sasha. Only a handful of people in the world had an inkling of their capabilities. And maybe no one, not even the scientists at the Animal Intelligence Initiative, understood their full potential.

Mulling over the dogs' abilities brought to mind the two children, Avi and Noah. Seven had to admire how they had outsmarted him at almost every turn. He silently toasted them as he remembered their interactions with him. They were as different from typical children as Sasha and Ajax were from regular German Shepherds.

Seven put his drink aside as a chill raced down his spine. He took out his iPad and booked a seat on the next plane to Boston.

The Academy

Noah, Avi, Sasha, and Ajax reached the meeting spot before Diego and Nico. Although the weeks following the Faction's downfall had been surprisingly uneventful, this was the first day they had been allowed to walk alone. Noah smiled as he watched Sasha walk next to Ajax. Avi looked at him with a raised eyebrow.

"So, what's going on in that head of yours, Noah?"

"I was thinking things feel like old times, but then I realized it's even better."

Avi playfully growled at Ajax before saying, "Easy for you to say. You didn't get kicked out of bed at 4:00 this morning."

"You need to get him his own bed like I did with Sasha."

"Noah, do you think it's really over? It was great none of the articles mentioned our names, but..."

"Well, Director Johnston had promised to keep our involvement quiet. I'm hoping this is it, but it seems hard to believe. And there's Seven. He's out there. I feel it."

Diego and Nico joined them. Diego was beaming, "Guess who got asked to participate in a special DRIA program this summer?"

Walking to the school's entrance, he told them all about the offer from Director Johnston. "I won't get paid anything, but I get access to the coolest technology. And talk about a resume builder!"

Kellen was waiting at the gate to take Sasha and Ajax to the lab. Tapping his watch, he said, "You guys are going to be late again." The group watched the two canines and Kellen walking away. Nico glanced at Noah and asked, "Has Sasha gained some weight?"

The Center

Jens and Indira sipped coffee in her office. She patiently waited for him to break the silence. After five minutes, she blurted out, "It's hard to believe we weren't mentioned prominently in any of the articles!"

"Indira, this is a good thing. We want to stay out of the public eye."

"I agree. It's just strange. We were kidnapped! And then the whole affair is portrayed as something else."

The two of them sat in silence for a minute before she added in a quiet voice, "Do you think anyone has caught on to our other project?"

Jens thought before he spoke. "Activities like this certainly increase the risk of exposure. I'm wondering how long it will take before they figure it out themselves."

"Do you think we should tell them?"

"Yes. Very soon. I think they are ready."

Indira nodded and took a sip of coffee. "What do you think will happen if others find out?"

"They will be taken away." He thought for a moment. "We have the resources. Maybe it's time to relocate."

Before she could answer, Kellen knocked and poked his head into the room. His smile went from ear to ear.

"Kellen, you seem ready to burst. What is it?"

"Sasha and Ajax have huge news!"

AUTHOR'S NOTE

The Protectors is a work of fiction. The characters in this book are all created from the author's imagination. Any resemblance to actual persons living or dead is coincidental. While some of the government agencies are real, such as the National Science Foundation and Department of Defense, they have been used fictitiously. The Deployable Operations Group previously existed, but it is no longer in operation. The Defense Research Intelligence Agency and the National Technology Security Council do not exist to the author's knowledge. Similarly, the Faction and Separatist Northwest are fictional.

Most of the locations used in the book are fictitious. Notable exceptions are the Colonial Inn and Old North Bridge Visitor Center in Concord, MA. In some cases, actual airports, such as Providenciales International Airport, and islands, such as North Caicos and Providenciales in the Turks and Caicos archipelago, have been portrayed. However, the events, people, and surroundings of these locations described in the novel are all from the author's imagination.

The author is not aware of any research programs, such as the Animal Intelligence Initiative or the Center, described in the book.

Similarities to any actual facility are coincidental.

Technology that enables modifications of genomes and the possibility of genetically modified species does exist. The author is not an expert on these technologies and is not making a statement against or supporting such efforts. *The Protectors* is meant to be a work of entertainment and should be read accordingly.

ABOUT THE AUTHOR

Paul Westgate is a business consultant turned author. He has a Ph.D. in Chemical Engineering and has held a wide range of professional roles from Research and Development to Business Leadership. He and his wife, Lori, live in Delray Beach, Florida.

Together, they have launched For Paws Media, LLC. www.forpawsmedia.com, a company dedicated to creating animal-oriented entertainment content and returning a portion of the proceeds to various not-for-profit organizations that are focused on animal causes.

ACKNOWLEDGEMENTS

Thank you to all of my friends and family who listened to this idea and patiently waited for it to come to fruition. A special note of appreciation goes out to our friend, Marlaya, who read early drafts. My greatest thanks are to my wife, Lori, who helped with every step of the book. I couldn't have done it without her.

Cover photos by Marek Szturc on Unsplash.

Made in the USA
Columbia, SC
02 May 2022

59539767R00165